In school when I had the chance to reread the exercise paper I had labored over for Mrs. Owens, and to my jaundiced eye it was passionless, unemotional, it was dead. I tried to tell you, Mrs. O., I thought; when I stick to prescribed form and structure, the magic dies. Without inspiration, there can be no art, and this . . . slaving . . . kills any magic that does come.

It started happening; the magic started coming back, swallowing me into the half-consciousness of a waking dream. I couldn't lose—what had Ken once called it?—the mustard seed of magic. I was more afraid of the bleakness of life without it than I was of what Miss Sadie would say if she caught me doing private writing in my notebook instead of listening to her English class.

The fourth book in the Keeping Days series

A Mustard Seed of Magic

a novel by
NORMA JOHNSTON

tempo
books
GROSSET & DUNLAP
A Filmways Company
Publishers • New York

FOR MITZI

as a mustard seed

December

O N   N E W   Y E A R ' S   E V E ,   1901, we all danced
at Stella Molloy's. All the crowd part of my
world—Celinda, and Stella's brother Larry, Anne
Cameron, Mike Felsen, Stella and my older brother
Ben. Marnie, my next younger sister, and Jimmie
Breidenbach from next door. Junius Albright, my sister
Bronwyn's stepson, whom I'm trying to draw into the
crowd, and even Mary Lou Hodge, making her first
reappearance after last year's big scandal. And
Kenneth—Kenneth, my friend, my love. We danced by
twos, in waltzes, and in groups through the old round
dances and the reels. Swing your partner and cast off,
bow to your corner and whirl with your opposite, till all

3

the pairings were broken down and the people intermixed . . . and then back again to home.

The old country dances were Mrs. Molloy's idea. She doesn't favor prolonged twosomes any more than my own mother does, but she hasn't caught on yet that the architecture of their sprawling old house is admirably suited for thwarting such parental ideas. Actually, Stella's New Year's party was my idea. Mama thought I ought to have one at my own house—and there's humor in that too, Mama actually urging a party, and my not wanting it. But this was Kenneth's last night as our houseguest before he went back on New Year's Day to his new Pennsylvania home. I emphatically didn't want to spend it spreading myself as thin as the jelly filling of Mama's Poverty Cake, being sweet and kind and hospitable to all and sundry. I wanted to spend it with Ken. Since Mama is not about to tolerate such single-minded intensity—especially as Mary Lou's similar involvement with Ken's brother Doug led to the infant currently being passed off as her baby brother—the Molloy's house, with its convenient butler's pantry, seemed best.

But all my planning seemed to have gotten me nowhere that night. I adore holidays, particularly Christmas, and I was absolutely ecstatic about Kenneth's visit. But something, ever since he came, had been driving me deeper and deeper into a Slough of Despond. The whole of Christmas Day had been a magic time. But all of Christmas week, despite the sugarplum excitement of parties and snowball fights, of sleighrides down the hill and skating on the pond—despite the intoxication of Ken's presence—had been an accelerating descent into despair. That was what was so disturbing: that this was happening to me while Kenneth

4

still was there. It troubled him, I know it did; he could not understand, and I could not explain.

I was trembling with cold when I got dressed for the party at twilight on New Year's Eve. It was perfectly ridiculous, too, for Ben had just heaved coal prodigally into the furnace, and steam was clanking cosily in the heating pipes. The water pipes were gurgling, too, as Ken got his turn with the bathtub down the hall. I thought again, as I had every day that week, how queer it seemed to have one's beau sharing the same plumbing, hearing the same family rows. And then it struck me that this was the last time I could think that way, for goodness knows how long, and all at once the luminous purple outside my window turned to night.

There was a tap on my door, and my sister Bron stepped in. "I've come to do your hair up for the party," she said. "We're having dinner here, you know, so I thought Saranne and I would just come on early and help you out." And then, in some surprise, "Why, Tish, you're crying!"

"No, I'm not," I said flatly. "I've got something in my eye."

Bron's eyes searched me, but she let that pass. She laid my niece, who's also my goddaughter, on the bed and turned round, smiling. "What are you wearing, the green velvet from my wedding? I'd better lace you tighter. The waist on that was small a year ago, and you've grown since then. Though I could swear that you look thinner, lately." Her tone was probing, but I did not respond. I presented my corset strings for her to tug, slid into the velvet dress she held for me, sat down on the dressing table bench so she could pile my hair up in a pompadour.

"You really do look like a young lady now," Bron

said. "It's hard to realize you're going on sixteen. And I'm almost twenty, and a mother, with a teen-age stepson! *O tempore!*"

"New Year's Eve's *supposed* to mark the passing of time," I said lightly. But after she left, I stood surveying myself soberly in the bureau mirror. The pompadour was becoming, and the camomile rinse I'd been using had given my dirty-blonde hair golden lights. My skin is golden, too, like all of us Sterlings, an inheritance from a mythical Indian ancestor, and my lashes, fortunately long, cast shadows underneath my eyes. They weren't red, but they showed I had been crying, and I did look thinner. I did look older. Time was passing.

That was the trouble, wasn't it? Just as I was pulled between practicality and dreaminess, between my sensitivity and the callousness I can unfortunately display, so was I pulled between a yearning to be grown-up, and a deep need to have time stand still, to hold tight to everything that was dear and precious to me lest it be forever lost.

I could not hold onto Kenneth, who had moved away with his family to his uncle's farm in Pennsylvania. His mother could not face living in West Farms any more, not since the Doug Latham–Mary Lou Hodge affair, which was ever-present in everybody's minds, even while we pretended it had never happened. Hypocrisy or kindness? I didn't know, and I no longer even cared. But I hated Doug Latham for what his sins were doing to us all.

My grandfather had had a farm in Pennsylvania, near Ken's uncle's, which I dearly loved. But Gramps was dead now, and the farm was sold. Change, as my father has all too often pointed out, is a fact of life.

6

Mouth-watering odors were emanating from the kitchen—Mama, who loathes cooking, is a very good cook, and since she hadn't had to go to work that week, and she had been cooking instead of Marnie and me, our dinners had decidedly improved. The front door slammed; I heard my brother-in-law Sidney Albright speaking to Pa. Saranne started yelling just to be sociable. Katie, my year-old sister, was likewise exercising her lungs. Feet tramped up the stairs, a fist banged on the bathroom door. "Hey, Latham," Ben called, "I know you're company, but can I remind you Marnie and I have to get cleaned up for the party too?" And Ken's voice answering, the door opening, Marnie muttering something about a possible shortage of hot water, Ben responding he hoped for her sake that was not the case, the snap of her swatting him with a towel, which, from the sounds of outrage Ben gave forth, was wet.

"You children get a move on!" Mama hollered up. "No consideration for proper dinner hour, don't know why I bother, no appreciation. . . ." All the familiar, only-half-meant grumbling, and then Bron's soothing murmur and Mama's chuckle. The house was warm, the house was filled with life, and I stood in my room looking at my own reflection and felt alone and cold.

I decided I had better go downstairs and join the human race.

So I descended, and Mama took one look and had a few words to say about my festival attire. "Could have waited till after supper to put on that get-up. Can't fool me, thought being decked out in velvet would provide a good excuse for not helping, didn't you? I was a fool to ever give in and let you have Kenneth come."

Since inviting Kenneth for the holidays had been Mama's own magnificent idea, that was decidedly unfair, and unfortunately I made the mistake of saying so. Mama drew herself up taller, breathing fire.

"That's right! Try to do something nice for you, all the thanks I get! *My* vacation this week, too, you know! Might exert yourself once in a while to act as hostess, either off flitting hither and yon, or somewhere sulking. Not ingratiating yourself with *him* any, acting that way, let me tell you."

"Oh, hell and damn!" I exploded, borrowing Marnie's favorite expression. Mama had touched on a spot that was all too sore. My mood was not fair to Kenneth, and well I knew it. "I guess it *was* a mistake to have Ken come. There, I've said it. Are you satisfied?"

"We *are* in a mood," Marnie said, coming down for the buttermilk with which she sought to bleach some freckles from her face. In the past few months, Marnie has suddenly become concerned about things like that. With her almost-black hair and Mama's snapping eyes, Marnie is beginning to resemble Bronwyn's beauty, and that too stirred an uncomfortable mixture of feelings in me.

"If you don't like my mood, just let me alone," I retorted. Marnie opened her mouth to respond, and then we stopped abruptly. Kenneth was standing behind her in the hall. He looked rather pale, and he avoided our eyes, speaking to my mother.

"Mrs. Sterling, could I trouble you to help me with this tie?" His voice was low and courteous. Ken has beautiful manners, and indeed this diversionary tactic could be classed among them, since I knew that he was capable of tying his own dress ties. Mama sailed over to him wordlessly, and when she had finished he thanked her quietly and departed, and Marnie flushed and vanished, too. Mama said only, "Hope you're satisfied,

8

miss," and went back to rattling kettles, and I went to set the table, wondering with a sinking feeling just how much Ken had overheard.

Thank goodness, I thought, for Pa's and Ben's conversational contributions during dinner. Ken and I, as dinner progressed, grew quieter and quieter. I was very glad the dinner hour was short.

Then it was time to leave for Stella's party. Jimmie arrived from next door, stamping off snow, to escort my sister. Kenneth fetched my coat and held it for me politely, but his hands didn't linger on my shoulders as they usually did. He held the door open, and I went out, down the icy steps. We walked in silence, side by side, but something held me back from tucking my arm through his.

I guess it was a mistake to have Ken come. How could I have said it? Even when, especially when, it could be all too true. But not for the reasons Kenneth might imagine. Not because I didn't want him, but because I wanted him too much. Because having him here this short week, had made all the more unbearable the fact that in another day he would be gone.

Lights glowed from every window of the Molloys' house, and a burst of music greeted us as we went up the path. Stella had received several new gramophone rolls for Christmas, and they were being put to use. There were bursts of laughter from the double parlors and Stella, when she greeted us, was flushed and glowing. "Come on in! You know where to put your things. There's hot cider in the dining room. Make yourselves at home." Her smile flashed, but her eyes were on my brother, and in no time she had Ben, who claims he has two left feet, dancing with her.

I went upstairs to take off my coat in Stella's room

and encountered Celinda Dodds, wearing her new sky-blue party dress, the first she'd ever owned, and looking like Cinderella at the ball. She took one look at me, and her eyes darkened. "Tish, what's the matter?"

"Matter? Who says anything's the matter?" I responded with what I hoped was airy nonchalance.

"Don't try that with me," Celinda said quietly. "I've known you since we were four, remember? You've been miserable all week; everybody knows it. I wish you'd tell me why. I wish you'd let us help."

"*I* wish people would stop trying to take my temperature every two minutes and let me alone."

Celinda shut her eyes briefly and then left without a word while I gazed after her, feeling as if I should cut out my tongue. I took my coat off, fluffed the flounces of my point lace yoke, pinched my cheeks to bring the color to them, and went downstairs. The gaiety of the party struck me like a blow.

Looking down on it, from the detachment of the staircase, was like seeing a great spreading tapestry, a whole composed of many tiny scenes. Stella and Celinda with their heads together. Ben, dancing with Mary Lou Hodge in her bright red dress. Ken sitting quietly by the fireplace watching them—or trying not to, rather. Ken, looking as if he too wondered if it would have been better if he had not come.

I went down the stairs straight to Kenneth, and I plastered a smile across my face. I said, "I've come back. I've swept the cobwebs out."

It may have been an ambiguous statement, but Ken knew what I meant. His eyes searched me, but he took the hands I held out to him and swept me into the dance. Glory, it felt good to shut my eyes and have no need to think. We didn't speak. The music moved us, carried us on, through the waltz and then the country dances Stella's mother introduced to disperse the pairs. We separated, came together once again, ate chicken salad and cupcakes and drank hot spiced cider. The music was warming and joyful, but underneath it was like the ticking of a clock, moving us relentlessly to the coming of 1902.

"Choose your partners for the grand reel," Mrs. Molloy called firmly. Kenneth took my hands and led me into place. We were first; we kept getting moved up closer toward the wall as other couples joined us. Mrs. Molloy sat down at the piano and launched zestfully into "Turkey in the Straw."

I have to admit I love the Virginia Reel. I have ever since we were first maneuvered through it at dancing class. I've danced it with Ben, I've danced it with Pa, I danced it with Kenneth in Pennsylvania when I was staying with Gramps and he was working at his uncle's farm. So I had no qualms about our being the head couple; I could have led off in my sleep, and so could Ken. So when Mrs. Molloy, with a flourish, sent forth those irresistible notes, I pranced out gaily—and found myself almost bumping noses with Junius Albright.

You don't do all the preliminary skirmishes with your own partner, but with your opposite number down at the far end of the line. It was not improbable that the Last Gent should turn out to be Junius; Mrs. Molloy had probably dragged him into the line-up by sheer force. And his partner—oh, horror—the Last Lady with whom Ken would have to do the bowing, the do-si-do-ing, the both-hands-round—was Mary Lou Hodge.

All this registered upon me, as the novelists would say, in the twinkling of an eye. And then I was curtseying to Junius's bow, bouncing back to place, Ken and

Mary Lou were confronting each other in the proper form, just as if nothing under the sun was wrong.

Just as if facing Junius, on a night I was all wrapped up with Ken, didn't for some ridiculous reason make me feel that I was hurting him, just because I'd tried to be friends with him. Just as if Mary Lou's ordeal in dancing with Doug's brother—not to mention that brother going through it with Doug's discarded girl—didn't flood Ken with vicarious guilt down to the bottom of his soul.

Patterns. Recurring patterns. I had never been so vividly conscious of them before. Ken and I. I and Junius. Ken and his deep pity for Mary Lou. Ken and Doug, Mary Lou and Doug; the specter of that blasted good-for-nothing hovered like a black cloud above us. And all the other patterns—Stella who was stuck on Ben; Ben's surprising compassion for Mary Lou whom he used to so despise. Celinda's compassion tonight for Kenneth. . . .

We finished the preliminaries and Kenneth and I came together, swinging once and a half around to commence the actual Reel.

Right to your partner, left to your corner. Ken and I meeting, separating, meeting again to part . . . round and about, swinging down the line, I with each gent in turn, he with each lady, always together again in center to twist round and spin off once more. Like lacing a pair of shoes, like skating very fast at night on thin ice when the wind was stinging cold. It wasn't cold here, though, it was very hot. The music got faster and louder, and my breath burned in my chest.

I felt as if this reel was never going to end, as if Ken and I would go on being flung in and out of it forever. But that wasn't true, for Ken was going off tomorrow, leaving me alone. To pick up the pieces of my unkind-ness to Mama and Celinda, to Junius whom I lately had led on, whether I wanted to admit to that or not.

The silly false grin on my face grew stiffer, and my breathing faster, and the pain in Ken's eyes and behind Mary Lou's bravado grew stronger, and I could have wept for all of us.

But there was a detachment in me, too. For even as I moved through the patterns, coming together and separating from Ken and from the others, my other prac-tical half stood off and watched, said I was wallowing in the extravagance of my own emotions. Even as I ached for the others (and let's face it, for myself), that other half was saying this was all wonderful material to write a story about some day.

I felt like a ghoul; I felt like a cannibal.

That was why I'd been behaving so unloveably, feel-ing so unloving and unloved. Why, as Marnie said, I "had a mad on" for everyone. The person I really had a mad on for was me. Practicality and sensitivity; I couldn't put the two halves of me together. I didn't know if I ever could, without Ken as the balance I had discovered he could be. I'd learned to survive without Ken's presence over the fall, and it had been good for me, much as I loathe to say so. But having him come back had taught me the extent to which I'd missed him. It had been like having the scab pulled off a half-healed wound. I didn't know whether I could go through the congealing process once again.

So my feet moved, my face smiled, my arms reached out to one and to another, and my one thought was, I must keep going, I mustn't disgrace the family, mustn't ruin Ken's last night here.

All at once my sides hurt from holding back those

blasted, unwanted sobs. Only two more gents to go, and now Ken and I were clasping hands in a grip so tight it hurt. We were sliding up the center, going round outside, forming a bridge for the others to tunnel under.

We were foot couple now, and had to go through the whole fool thing again. And all of a sudden I simply couldn't do it. I tried, I'd swear on a stack of Bibles that I did. But as Stella, the next Head Lady, came swishing down towards Ken, a sob escaped me, and the tears spilled, and I bolted. I ran, unthinkingly, blindly, to the dimness of the big old butler's pantry.

How long I remained there in the darkness I do not know, but it must have been a good long time, enough for two changes of the Reel at least. Then the swinging door banged, and Stella stood beside me. "All right," she said without preamble, "what's the matter now?"

It was the word *now* that smote me. "Stella Molloy, if you came out here to lecture me, you can just not bother. You can just go right back inside."

"It's my house," Stella retorted. "You needn't tell me what to do in it. Which, come to think of it, you did with this whole party. You were the one who wanted it, remember, so you and Ken could have one last big happy time together? Well, excuse me for saying so, but you don't seem to be working at it very hard."

"Maybe I'm working at it *too* hard. I just can't ever forget that it *is* the last."

"What you can't forget," Stella said deliberately, "is that blasted sensitivity of yours. You check its pulse every five minutes. Did it ever occur to you that it could be sheer self-indulgence? Or dramatizing?"

Saying that last was like waving a red flag at a bull, and Stella had meant it to be exactly that. I stared at her, white-faced. But before I could breathe fire, she turned on her heel and was gone.

I felt like heaving after her a good heavy hunk of glass. What I did reach for was the nearest unbreakable object, which turned out to be a wooden spoon, and lobbed it toward the flour-barrel. I knew perfectly well that I was acting Melissa's age, and that knowledge did not exactly contribute to my peace of mind.

To my horror, an apparition rose before my eyes, an apparition with all too familiar scarecrow ears, gingerly rubbing a flour-spattered brow.

"Junius Albright," I demanded when I could speak, "what in the name of all suffering saints are you doing eavesdropping on a private conversation?"

"When a fellow's already in a quiet corner," Junius replied with dignity, "how's he to know two females would choose the same spot for a catfight?" The blood drummed in my ears, and he gave me one of his rare direct looks. "Yes, I figured you'd be here. I'd had enough of the howling mob, too, and I thought maybe later you'd need a listening ear. Then Stella materialized playing the Scourge of God." He shrugged and reached for something on the floor beside him. "If you splashed some water on your face, you might feel better."

I went to the soapstone sink and followed his suggestions, hoping it would quell the telltale crimson of my cheeks. Behind me, in the dimness, came an unexpected *pling,* a *plong,* and then to my astonishment a cascade of silvery notes. I whirled around, flabbergasted.

"I never knew you played a guitar!"

"I don't really. I just pick at it. Aunt Sadie thinks it's a stupid waste of time." Now it was Junius who flushed. He said hurriedly, "This is Larry's. I saw it in

15

the hall. I don't cart mine around." His fingers started a run of melody, then stopped. "No, that's the wrong mood." The notes began again, an intricate off-beat tapestry of sound, plaintive and poignant.

"Do you mean to say," I managed shakily at last, "that you can play like that and you've never told a soul?"

"A fellow doesn't want to be a trained seal," Junius said quietly. "Especially when he's enough of a circus exhibition anyway."

"Junius," I said slowly with more accuracy than tact, "you're a prize fool. Here you worry about not being accepted in the crowd, when you've got in your hands the best key you could hope to have. If you can play like that, you can play for folks to sing with, can't you?"

"Sure, but—"

"Never mind the buts. That's just what we all could use now."

Junius nodded. "I just thought," he said heavily. "If *you* left the Reel, and *I* left, that means Ken and Mary Lou had to dance together, didn't it?"

It was a realization that was only just occurring to my own mind.

Somewhere in the front of the house, a clock began to chime. The beginning of the new year, 1902. Ken was in there, thinking Lord knows what, and I was in the pantry with Junius feeling sorry for myself. Oh, there were a lot of New Year's resolutions I had better make, but not just now. I grabbed Junius's hand.

"Come on. And don't you dare not bring that guitar!"

We emerged into the double parlors, which were still filled with movement, but Kenneth's eyes were lifted

16

straight to mine, and there was an unfathomable expression in them.

I didn't even stop to think. I dropped Junius's hand and sped straight through the crowd to Kenneth. "Happy New Year," I said. "*All* of them. Ken, Junius is going to play so we can sing."

One of the blessed things about Kenneth is that he never needs prompting to pick up cues. Before we knew it, Ken had everyone sitting around the fireplace, and the flames leaped up the chimney as our voices joined.

> *For auld lang syne, my dears,*
> *For auld lang syne,*
> *We'll drink a cup of kindness yet*
> *For auld lang syne. . . .*

If there was a lump in my throat, I did not allow myself to dwell upon it. The rest of the party was warm and gay and ended only when the parent Molloys drove us at last firmly out into the night. We walked home in groups, laughing and singing, and I didn't have a further chance for introspection. But when I was home, beneath three blankets in my room alone, the words of the song came back.

A cup of kindness. I'd been so wrapped up in what was, or soon would be, that I hadn't given much thought at all to kindness. Phrases from the prayer we say in church each Sunday floated to my mind. I had indeed "done those things we ought not to have done, and left undone" things that ought to have been my primary concern.

The house was very still, but I was too wide-awake and too keyed-up for sleep. I hugged the blankets to me as outside my window a soft steady rain began to fall. A pot of tea, that was what I needed, the warmth and comfort of a pot of tea.

After the upstairs chill, the kitchen was welcoming and cosy. I shut the doors prudently, lit the lamp, and threw wood on the stove. I was trying to be very quiet, but just as the kettle was coming to a boil the hall door opened and Kenneth came in. He, too, had obviously had trouble sleeping.

"I thought that you were here." He took the teapot from me and began to measure tea. I sat down in Mama's rocker, hoping that if any of my family stirred they would have the blessed tact not to come down.

The hanging lamp cast a soft glow round the familiar room, and Ken's eyes followed it. "I love your kitchen," he said, drawing up a chair across from me. "It has such a feel of home."

There was a silence while a log cracked in the stove. Ken poured the tea and we sat sipping it in quiet.

"Ken," I said at last, "I don't want you to go."

"I don't want to," he responded. "You know that, don't you? But maybe you were right when you said it would have been better if I hadn't come." He stirred his cup while the words hung in the air. "That wasn't one of our better parties tonight, was it?"

"I'm sorry about leaving you to dance with Mary Lou. I wasn't thinking—that is, I was thinking just of me."

"Maybe it was just as well. The Hodges and the Lathams can't avoid each other always, so that's one hurdle that we're now across." Ken sighed. "I still hate the thought of not living here, but Mother can't bear the sight of anyone from West Farms. Tonight, for the first time, I could understand."

18

We gazed at each other, and I said, "I know. Ken, I do miss talking to you so."

"There are always letters. You write good letters."

"Even if they make being away that much harder on you?"

"Even so." Ken was silent for a moment. "I think I didn't write more because I was jealous, in a way. There's so little I can do—for you, for anyone. The farm's dead in winter, and my parents . . . I just sort of sit around the house and rot. I wish I had things I had to do, like you do. You broke a lot of ice, getting Junius to play that guitar tonight."

"It gave me a respectable way to reappear, too, after my grand exit. But I swear to goodness I wasn't thinking of that at the time."

Ken laughed. "That's your blessing and your curse. You never do calculate results beforehand, you just act from the heart."

"Maybe it would be better sometimes if I didn't."

Ken's grin vanished. "No, it wouldn't. You'd be losing a part of yourself. A part that's a special gift."

"Some gift, if it ends up hurting people."

That was supposed to come out rueful laughter, but I didn't quite succeed. Ken poured more tea and put his hand on mine across the table.

"It *is* 'some gift.' You're very lucky, you know. You've got something that you have to do, that won't ever let you go, and that makes all the difference." I just looked at him, and he reached over and picked up an object lying on the table and put it in my hand, closing my fingers round it.

A pencil. One of those familiar, stubby yellow pencils we all use in school, that I always have pocketed somewhere with scraps of paper for scribbling down my thoughts.

"Your writing," Ken said. "You have a means of speaking to other people, whether they are able then to hear or not. You make them feel and make them understand. Whether that's a blessing or curse, or both, is irrelevant. What matters is to keep doing it, because you have to, and to do it the very best you can."

"Kenneth," I said slowly, "I do love you."

"And I you." Laughter glimmered somewhere in the back reaches of his eyes. He came around the table, and he kissed me.

I have a lot of New Year's resolutions to make tomorrow, after Kenneth goes.

January

O NCE THE CHRISTMAS holidays were over, life very rapidly went back to normal. Or turned to chaos, rather, which is the exact same thing. Pa has been known to refer to our household not as a menage but a menagerie.

On Wednesday, the first of January, 1902, we had New Year's dinner down at Albrights'. I tried to get Junius to play his guitar, but he would not; he got quite cross at my even mentioning it to Bron and Sidney. I was going to have to do something about that, I thought. But not yet, not today. Pa started talking that afternoon about going back to work at the secretarial school, which got Mama and Bron and Aunt Kate all quite perturbed. They said his eyes were not yet recovered enough from the operation. I started a new journal. And Kenneth left.

Kenneth left directly after dinner, with Sidney driving him alone down to the station. Pa and Mama didn't give us much choice on the subject, but it was all right; we had said everything we could say to each other the night before. A tight embrace, a kiss when no one could see, a last look into each other's eyes, and then he went his way and I went mine. And if I was very silent the rest of the afternoon, the family tactfully made no comment.

Later, we all scattered to our own affairs. Ben departed to points unknown. Mama was in Pa's study with the door closed; I could hear the soft rising and falling of their voices. Marnie went skating at the pond with Jimmie Breidenbach. Katie was sleeping in the cradle by the fire, and Melissa was taking advantage of Katie's naptime to spread her coloring books in safety on the floor.

I made myself a pot of tea, and took it upstairs to the sanctuary of my room. I'd been wanting for hours to be alone to write, but once I was there in blessed solitude I couldn't think of anything to say. My thoughts were too tangled and confused to pin down in words. I looked at the new journal, with its tantalizingly empty pages, and lay back on my pillows and all I could think was that Ken was right, the ties do bind between us despite time and space, and I do have a blessing. I *am* a writer, I will always have to write, nothing—not my own doubting, not family amusement nor Miss Sadie Albright's notable lack of appreciation of my compositions—can wipe that out. My choice, as Ken had said, was only how I used it.

I was going to learn to use it well and wisely. That was one of my firm resolutions for the new year.

Another was to be kinder to Junius, help him with his music. Help Mary Lou get back into the crowd without that invisible scarlet letter we involuntarily kept seeing on her bosom. Think more about others' needs and less about my own. Learn to use my writing as a means of reaching out to others, and stop being so blasted protective of it for fear of being misunderstood.

I ought to write them down, I thought. But the words didn't come. All I put down, in black ink on the fresh white pages, was, "Praise God from whom all blessings flow." Which was a pretty strange thing for me to be saying, considering the state of mind I'd been in lately. Considering Kenneth had just gone. It was such a good feeling I wanted to hug it to my heart and never let it go.

The feeling spilled over into the next day when we all went back to school. Mama was bustling about six ways from Sunday, sitting down to spoon porridge into Katie with her hat already pinned onto her head. It didn't seem queer any more to have Mama going off to work. It even seemed natural, heaven help us, to have Aunt Kate stalking in the back door with an armful of books and newspapers to read aloud to Pa. Pa's eyes were much better now, but he still was not allowed to read, nor go back to work, and he was decidedly chafing at the bit.

"Don't think of it," Mama said, correctly interpreting the look upon Pa's face. "Not setting foot in that school till eyes are good and ready. Relapse all we need. Don't go wheedling Doc Tuttle, either, behind my back. *He* might be softheaded enough, think you could go back and not use your eyes, but I know better."

She popped into her good grey coat and picked up a pile of corrected shorthand papers in one arm and Katie in the other, preparatory to depositing her for the day at Bron's. "I'll get home early if I can. You young folks

23

figure out whose turn it is to get supper. One disadvantage eating out yesterday, no leftovers to heat up.'' She sailed out, feeling no end smug, I swear, about being able to leave a kitchen full of dirty dishes behind her with clear conscience.

"Jimmie's waiting for me,'' Marnie announced hastily, diving for the door. There were people waiting for me, too, but I couldn't leave plates of congealing porridge to await our mid-afternoon return. I picked up the dish towel reluctantly.

Pa smiled whimsically. "You run along. I'll do 'em today. Guess that's one thing at least won't strain these confounded eyes.''

Aunt Kate looked scandalized, but I didn't catch her offering to pitch in. As for me, I closed my ears to my conscience and sallied forth gratefully into the cold bright morning. Stella and Celinda were already at the corner. Celinda took one look and her eyes crinkled with amusement.

"What happened? We were expecting a wake, but you look as if you have a Fourth of July sparkler going off inside of you!''

"I'm happy,'' I said. "I'm so happy I could just burst. I just know it, things are going to happen. . . . Race you up the hill!'' And we were off, pelting helter-skelter, to fetch up breathless and glowing on the next corner.

"I can tell you one thing's going to happen,'' Stella said, trying ineffectually to repair damage to her tumbled hair. "Mary Lou's returning to the bosom of the West Farms educational establishment. Which is not one bit happy about it.''

"What!''

"Fact. Mr. Hodge telephoned my father last night to

ask if he could come up to the house to consult him, holiday or no." Mr. Molloy was a lawyer, and Stella was undoubtedly spilling confidential information, but we listened shamelessly. "Mr. Hodge said Mary Lou'd set her heart on going back to school, and he knew the neighbors were not about to like it. He wanted to know if there was any way Mr. Moore, or the School Board, could keep her out. Father said he didn't see how they could, 'After all, there's a public record that it was *Mrs*. Hodge who recently had a baby,' so he didn't think they need worry."

"Imagine Mary Lou Hodge wanting to go to school," Celinda said. "She's not exactly known for scholarship. I should think it's the last thing she'd want to do."

"Maybe she's turned over a new leaf."

Stella snorted. "Can the leopard change his spots?" And we all laughed, but I had an uneasy feeling that something was not right, and that the trouble was with *us*, not Mary Lou.

I had that feeling again when we reached the girls' cloakroom at the school. As always, it was jammed just before the warning bell. Girls were fighting for a turn to primp before the one small mirror, and despite the fact that most of us had seen each other just a day or two before, everyone was talking a mile a minute about the holidays, when all of a sudden there was a silence. I happened to be before the mirror at that moment, and as I looked into it, I saw, reflected, Mary Lou standing in the cloakroom door, wearing an overtrimmed hat and her loud plaid coat.

There was a silence, and then everyone talked at once. Everyone turned to the nearest person and began to gabble, so there were a lot of little circles, protectively closing. In the old days Mary Lou used to be the obnoxious Queen Bee of the cloakroom, but now even her old crony Charlene didn't seem to know her from the woodwork. The only other person not swallowed up by those circles was myself. And even as I groaned inwardly, I heard my voice say, with too much brightness, "Hey, Mary Lou, you want the looking glass? I'm through with it."

Why oh why, does it always have to be me who gets stuck going out on limbs for the waifs and strays? Especially for Mary Lou, who so often made me feel like a waif and stray myself. I felt that way right then, as a matter of fact; I turned red and mumbled, "Cee, come on, we've got to find Mrs. Owens and ask what's happening next with the *Literary Magazine*."

"Whew!" Celinda said when we were safely down the hall. "Stella was right. There are going to be problems. That was awful."

"That won't be the half of it. I can just hear Miss Sadie, not to mention our Aunt Kate."

"All the pillars of virtue," Celinda said, with an unaccustomed viciousness that startled me. "Stella's wrong about one thing," she said after a pause. "People *can* change. If nothing else, you have to admire Mary Lou for having courage."

"It would help if she had a few less other things. If only I could *like* her a little," I said.

"Well," Celinda said quietly, "liking's kind of beside the whole point, really."

There are times when Celinda makes me painfully aware just how small and petty my own thoughts can be.

The school day was like all those that immediately follow a vacation. Teachers were muttering dark threats about the necessity for getting back down to work. Mr.

Moore assigned a major research paper. Mr. Moore is principal of our school, and a lovely person, but his return to the classroom to teach our history class during Mr. Grimes's leave of absence has been sheer disaster. He has been away from daily lessons for so long that he grossly overestimates the quantity of homework anyone can do. His assignments, especially when coupled with Miss Sadie's English ones, add up to sleepless nights if taken seriously. Since I had not taken any homework seriously enough during the two months before the holidays, I had some midnight oil to burn, as Mrs. Owens reminded me when I caught up with her at last at three o'clock.

"There will be an officers' meeting of Browning Society after school tomorrow." Mrs. Owens hesitated. "Tish, you are going to work harder this marking period, are you not? Mr. Moore asked me if you were going to pull your grades up enough to continue being secretary. He's been concerned about you, and so have I. Irresponsibility and not caring are so unlike you."

"I know. I'm sorry. I had a lot on my mind, but everything's all right now. I mean to do better, and I'll do more editorial work on the *Literary Magazine,* too, if you still want me."

"I *am* glad. You have a real gift, Tish, and therefore a responsibility to use it wisely." She smiled warmly and moved off down the hall. I stood there, struck by how close her words had been to what Ken had said.

Celinda appeared beside me. "I feel as if I already need another vacation. I get tired just looking at this list of work! Let's go down to the library, shall we, and start our history research?"

Today was Marnie's turn to start cooking dinner, so I accepted with alacrity. It felt good to be rummaging through the library with Celinda. In the bookstacks we encountered Anne and Stella on a similar mission and devoted ourselves to the Groves of Academe for a solid hour. Then Stella slapped a fat book shut and groaned. "If one more person reminds me that from now till Easter is three months of uninterrupted drudgery, I'm going to spit!"

"We've done enough labor for a first day's effort," Celinda said, as the librarian directed a dark glance in our direction. "Come over to my house and I'll make some tea. I've got a plum cake and a tin of Lapsang Souchong."

Celinda's becoming quite a housekeeper, especially since Larry's discovered gourmet and intellectual interests are not mutually exclusive. So we trooped over to Dodds', and the plum cake was very good, though I have to admit the tea reminded me of old charred rope. Stella liked it, though; she thought it had character.

Celinda laughed. "Larry did, too. It must be the staunch old Irish Catholic Puritanism in you Molloys. Anything's got to be astringent to be any good!"

"I'm not sure how much I'm—" Stella stopped, flushed, and unaccountably changed the subject. "There's a Browning Society meeting tomorrow afternoon, I hear. Do you suppose la belle Hodge will appear? Because if so, somebody'd better plan how to handle it. Another sticky situation like this morning we do not need."

"It's just an officers' meeting tomorrow," I said hastily, and Celinda added, "Anyway, you have to maintain an eighty average to stay an active member, and Mary Lou's never been noted for her brains."

"According to her papa, the dear girl has become a cloistered scholar." More of what Stella had overheard?

Anne looked up innocently. "I wouldn't think Mary Lou'd have the gall to come back into Browning Society, anyway. Wasn't there a big scandal once about her plagiarizing a poem?"

There had, indeed, and I'd been the one responsible for spilling the beans on that to the authorities. I dropped my eyes.

"Gall," Celinda said, "has never been a thing Miss Hodge is short of."

"Oh, my dears, if she starts being a conspicuous light around Browning Society, there's going to be the devil to pay. We all know Browning Society's a thorn in the flesh of a lot of folks, already. Too much encouraging youth to exercise critical faculties and think for itself," Stella added scathingly. "Look at the fuss when we put on *A Doll's House* last fall. People are riled up about that still, *and* about Mary Lou coming back to West Farms at all."

"She has a right to an education, if she wants one," I heard my own voice say.

"To education, yes," Stella retorted, warming to the argument. "But does she have the right to jeopardize Browning Society for the rest of us? If she had any sense, she'd play the shrinking violet for a while, but she certainly doesn't seem inclined to. She could put the rest of us, not to mention Mrs. Owens, in a very difficult situation. The question is, do we let her, or do we not?"

"Maybe," Celinda said with an edge of malice, "you'd better light a few candles at St. Catherine's that Mary Lou just not show up."

Stella didn't answer, but an odd expression crossed her face. I looked at her sharply, and then the front door opened, and a voice called, "Is anybody home?"

Stella scrambled to her feet with something like re-lief. "It's Larry. Did you come to walk me home?" she demanded, as her brother appeared in the parlor arch-way.

"Actually, I came to see if there was tea hot in the pot." Larry was looking at Celinda, and the current that passed between them made me feel, despite my sternest intention, suddenly lonely. I wondered, out of the blue, what Kenneth was doing. Reading at a library, walking home alone through country twilight? His school had reopened, too.

"There's Lapsang Souchong, and I've made a plum cake. I thought you might be by." Celinda's face was alight. "Larry, what is it? What did Mr. Moore have to say?"

"Don't tell me the genius got called to the princi-pal," Stella said with sisterly bite, and Larry grinned.

"Not in the sense you're meaning, sister dear. He's completed an evaluation of my records, the way he promised to do when we moved here. There was a ques-tion of where to put me when I switched schools, you remember, because I was between grade levels. Any-way, if I do two major research works this month, I can graduate the end of January and start at Columbia with the spring semester. Mr. Moore's been in touch with the admissions office, and it's all worked out."

In two seconds Celinda, the shy and unassertive, was across the room and hugging Larry hard. There were congratulations all around.

"You'll miss having a real graduation, though," Celinda said regretfully, and Larry shrugged.

"What do form and ceremony matter? I've learned all I can here; I'm eager to move on."

"We'll miss you around school," I said and saw a

shadow cross Celinda's face. Celinda would be in the same boat I was, now, though at least she would be able to see Larry outside of school. It startled me somewhat to realize how much Larry had become a part of our crowd, and of Celinda, in a short time. And how different, how much more human, he was, than we'd first thought—or else how much changed.

"Larry's a philosophy scholar," Stella said, swooping with the single-mindedness of a mosquito back to her earlier topic. "Larry, what is the ethical answer to the question of individual versus collective good? Meaning what do we do if Mary Lou shows up at Browning Society once again?"

The Dodds' mantel clock chimed six, and I jumped up. "If I don't reach home in two seconds flat, Mama will skin me, or else Marnie will."

There was a general exodus. It had been a pleasant afternoon, and I had a little virtuous glow at the thought of all the history research I'd accomplished. But beneath that glow there was a shadow. The gossip had been lovely fun, but I was left with an uneasy sense that we had voiced things that should not have been spoken.

I did not reach home in two seconds, but nobody lectured me. Marnie, flushed from standing over the kitchen range, looked very pretty and was not mad at all. This undoubtedly was attributable to the fact that Jimmie Breidenbach had appointed himself kitchen helper, with the evident intention of remaining to share our groceries. Melissa had set the table; the knives and forks were backward, but she was enormously proud of the job she'd done. And Peter, to my stupefaction, had produced a cake.

"He's old enough to pitch in, and had nothing to do with himself, so I said he might as well try. And it

31

turned out better'n ours do," Marnie said frankly. "Peter's better at things that take precision and concentration than either of us." She opened the oven and peered with satisfaction at her pork chops with cider and smothered apples. "I tell you, a few more months and we'll have this housekeeping down to a science!"

"Your Ma'll be back in the kitchen long afore that," Pa said, wandering in to sniff at the thyme and cinnamon. "You young folks have done a fine job, keeping things going, but I must say it'll feel good to me to have things back the way they ought to be, going to the school myself, your ma at home. Where *is* your ma, anyway?"

"Not to mention Ben. Those chops are going to cook bone dry if they don't show up soon." Marnie sounded so exactly like Mama that I choked back a laugh. "Where do you suppose that boy's been vanishing to lately?"

The front door opened with a gust of cold air, and Ben and Mama ambled in. Or rather, Ben ambled, Mama bustled at her usual brisk pace. Ben was being very gallant, carrying Mama's books and papers, helping her off with her coat, which meant he was trying to avoid questions about his own late arrival.

"What I'd like to know," Mama was saying. "Ought to be busy with school. Think about the future. Harvard. Not as if you had Doug Latham to get in trouble with no more."

"Then you don't have to worry, do you, Mama? By golly, a fellow likes some privacy—"

"Getting home after dark, family waiting to say grace together—"

"Kind of late yourself, aren't you, Evie?" Pa said mildly.

32

"Taste of your own medicine," Mama said, unpinning her hat. "Kept meals hot for you often enough, when school was getting started. Must say it feels good, come home find meal waiting for me 'stead of other way round. Edward Sterling, you know you're not supposed to strain your eyes!" She snatched away the pile of shorthand papers Pa was peering at.

"That cataract operation was designed to improve my eyes, not eliminate their use forever." Pa sounded irritated. "I can at least look things over. How do I know that new shorthand teacher's correcting papers as carefully as I would do?"

" 'Cause I have him make me up answer sheets, and I double-check," Mama retorted. "Not quite a fool. Kind of fun; almost feel like taking up shorthand myself."

"Wonders will never cease," I wrote that night in my journal. "Imagine Mama starting to like going out to business, at her age! I wish I could have had a picture of Pa's face."

I closed my journal and decided I'd better give some attention to Sourpuss Sadie's English composition assignment. But try as I might to stick within Miss Sadie's sterile guidelines, I kept bumping into things I wanted to say better; bumping into things I didn't want to see, things I certainly didn't want Miss Sadie Albright to observe. The fact was, I could not write for Sadie Albright, not anything that felt good to me. Oh drat and blast, I thought, flinging my writing tablet across the room, people like her shouldn't be allowed to give writing assignments. And people like me shouldn't have to write if they couldn't be honest.

I got up early in the morning and managed to squeeze out the required three pages, but I wasn't proud of it, or me. I wasn't proud of the fact that, hurrying late towards school, I saw Mary Lou walking ahead of me—also tardy—and deliberately held back, risking the late bell, so I wouldn't have to enter the school with her.

In classes, teachers were handing back papers corrected over vacation, and this did not add to my elation, especially when Miss Sadie handed back one of my walk-on-thin-ice, please-her-maintain-integrity-betray-nothing compositions with a red seventy. She added a verbal caustic comment about persons who regard themselves as literary prima donnas and aren't willing to be taught anything. Something snapped inside me, and I found I no longer cared what she thought. I'll show you, Sarah Albright, I thought; I'll be *danged* if I'm going to let you spoil my writing for me.

It was as though a load rolled off my back; as if suddenly I was freer to write than I had been in a long time; and all the rest of that day I was writing, writing, on notebook pages and sheets of composition pages hidden inside textbooks. All the tangled thoughts and feelings that had been going on inside me the past two days . . . I didn't know what I was going to do with them except that I *would* use them someday, some way, somehow.

At three o'clock I sailed into the Browning Society's officers' meeting on such a cloud of well-being that I found myself volunteering to write a skit to be done in assembly next week to solicit contributions to *Literary Magazine*.

"We only have three weeks before we go to press," Mrs. Owens pointed out. "Not to mention having the work out of the way before mid-term exams." That brought a general groan.

"Can't we do something between now and then to

enliven the social scene? Now that the play is over, everyone will lose interest if there's nothing exciting going on. And this part of the year is dull, dull, dull!''

"We ought to do something to raise money," the treasurer said firmly. "It's costing plenty to put out these extra issues of the magazine."

"What about the play?"

"Plays cost money, they don't make it. We need something fun and non-controversial."

"How about a Living Pictures Show? Scenes from great literature—all the books we're supposed to read, and don't. A last big bash the Friday night before exams begin."

"That's also our deadline day," the president pointed out. "And only three weeks away. There would be a lot of organization to do between now and then. Somebody who knows literature has to pick the scenes and pose the pictures."

With one accord, all heads turned toward Mrs. Owens.

"Doing *A Doll's House* took a great deal of out-of-school time, and I do have other . . . " Mrs. Owens hesitated, then capitulated. "Very well. As you say, it could be a good idea for many reasons."

Not for nothing is my family known for having foot-in-mouth disease. Before I knew it, I had volunteered to write a narration that would connect the various scenes together. When the meeting broke up, Mrs. Owens approached me, smiling. "Tish, I'm so glad you're back to doing creative writing once again."

"It's been a struggle," I said grimly. "Miss Albright's almost sunk the ship a couple of times already. All she cares about is form, not what the writer is trying to say."

35

"Even the most inspired writer," Mrs. Owens said drily, "has to submit to editing and to learn his craft."

"Yes, but you can't learn from somebody who has no feel—"A great thought struck me, and I rushed pell-mell into speech before I could turn coward. "Mrs. Owens, couldn't *you* work with me? Let me turn the things I write for myself in to you for comments I could trust?"

An odd look crossed Mrs. Owens's face. "Are you sure you want that? To have your work treated as serious writing, not school compositions?"

"Of course I do. I'm starved for it. What you said, about a writer having to learn the craft . . . I can't, not from somebody like Miss Albright. But I *can* learn from *you*. Won't you help me, please?"

Mrs. Owens stood looking at me for several seconds. "What you're asking . . . it's a different kind of thing from regular grading of papers against student norms. There's a kind of covenant involved, between a writer and an editor. The same as there is between an actor and director. They have to work together, there can't be a tug of war."

"I know that," I said, somewhat nettled.

"It can be merciless, and it can be brutal. But there can be no standard other than absolute honesty, and there can be no genuinely creative art without real encounter." Mrs. Owens's dark eyes met mine squarely. "You had better be very certain before you embark on such a project, Tish. For those are the only terms on which I could undertake it. Are you really certain you can take it?"

She didn't wait for my answer; she turned and left, as if deliberately giving me time to reconsider. I was shocked, and I was almost angry. I had not expected such unequivocal bluntness from gentle Mrs. Owens. But I knew, too, that this was something that I had to do.

I ought to have spent the weekend working on my history report, not to mention certain English homework, but I did not. I spent it wallowing in a cloud of inspiration. Ideas for the assembly skit pinwheeled through my mind all the time Marnie and I flew at Mama's heels through housework Saturday morning. Marnie was right, the house management was falling into a routine. And I was discovering something else as well—it was a lot more fun doing things with Mama now that Mama wasn't always around the house. She had things to talk about, and we had a good time gossiping about school matters, hers and ours, as we sailed through sheet-changing and furniture-polishing together. Mama had made one drastic change; she'd started sending out the laundry instead of killing herself over the washtubs and ironing board, and the difference that made in her disposition was marvelous to behold. Mama was also, I noticed, more willing to settle for licks and promises in the mop-and-broom department than she ever had been.

"Do best we can, all that can be expected. People more important than spit and polish," she said firmly.

"I hope some of this lasts once Mama's back to hearth and home again," Marnie murmured to me privately when Mama could not hear.

On Saturday afternoon, and again on Sunday, I drowned myself in a lovely orgy of ink. I wrote to Kenneth and told him about the skit, the Living Pictures Show, and my interview with Mrs. Owens. I wrote the skit. I started jotting down all sorts of ideas I was getting for the Living Pictures Show. And I was still in a fog when it was time to go down to Bron's for Sunday night Young People's meeting.

We were accompanied by Jimmie Breidenbach, who tagged along at Marnie's side. "Seems to me we're getting more ecumenical all the time," Ben commented, eyeing him. Jimmie was unabashed.

"Don't notice you objecting none to the Molloys coming," he said cheerfully. "We Catholics have to keep an eye on the competition, don't we?" The conversation ended abruptly as Ben stuffed a handful of wet snow down his neck. My brother does not appreciate teasing on the subject of Stella Molloy.

A burst of noise and music greeted us on the Albright threshold. Celinda was joggling Saranne, who should have been in bed but was obviously not in any mood for sleep, and Bronwyn was at the piano banging out hymns with a good crowd of singers gathered around. Sidney and Junius were distributing hot chocolate. The scene had just the kind of warmth and exuberance and good feeling that I loved. I parked my coat in the spare room and was just coming downstairs, feeling full of joy to the world, when two things happened.

The doorbell sounded, and when Junius opened it, Mary Lou Hodge walked in. At the same moment Mike Felsen spoke up from the couch where he was poking through the Sunday morning papers.

"Say, any of you fellows see this notice about a train wreck out West? There's a D. Latham listed among the injured. You don't suppose that could be *Doug* Latham, could it?"

Silence hung suspended. I was terribly conscious of the look on my brother's face, on Mary Lou's. Then Sidney was putting down his tray, saying easily, "Oh, I don't imagine so. Latham's really not an unusual name.

There's no point leaping to conclusion." My sister was swinging around on the piano stool, saying cordially, "Mary Lou, how nice to see you. Come along, I'll show you where to put your coat."

I could have offered to take Mary Lou up, but I didn't. I let them pass me on the stairs and didn't say a word.

Marnie came up beside me. "Sidney's right, you know," she said, looking at me shrewdly. "The West's a big place. Anyway, didn't Ken tell you Doug had found a job? He wouldn't still be bumming around on trains."

I hoped so. I certainly did hope so, for Kenneth's sake, and Ben's, and even Mary Lou's. Although I couldn't help involuntarily thinking some kind of an accident would serve Doug Latham right.

I went downstairs, with Marnie close beside me, and Ben went over and started talking about sports with Mike. After a while Bron and Mary Lou came back downstairs, and Sidney got a good discussion going. Bit by bit my happy mood returned. But that split-second moment lingered in my mind, and much later, when I was home in bed, it returned with such force that I could not shake it off.

The next day Mrs. Owens was pleased with the skit I had concocted. She didn't ask me, though, whether I had reconsidered my request for help with my real writing, and I did not speak of it. I would tell her my decision without the need for words.

It being my turn to cook dinner that week, I invited Celinda to come home for tea and keep me company. By the time we reached the house, our number had been augmented by Anne and Stella. I didn't put on the dog as much as Celinda'd done; we sat around the kitchen table while I threw a Stretchable Stew together. I also threw together some gingerbread, and this attracted Pa from his study, Ben and Larry from the attic, and Marnie and Jimmie Breidenbach from land-knows-where. The afternoon developed into an expanded version of our hen party at Celinda's house.

"We ought to do this regularly," Stella said. "You are hereby invited to the Molloy establishment the day after tomorrow."

"Why not tomorrow?"

"Because there's a Browning Society meeting then, remember? To give out *Literary Magazine* assignments and plan the Living Pictures Show."

It was a charming meeting. We had a gratifyingly large attendance. Everyone was already bored with school drudgery, and news of proposed social activities had spread. All the desks in Mrs. Owens's room were occupied, and there was a goodly representation perched on windowsills as well. I got there late, having been detained in the hall by Miss Albright, who had something to say about my rudeness in scribbling in my notebook all the time she'd been talking to the class.

"Not only is it extremely impolite, it is an example of wasted time and inattention, which you cannot afford." I gritted my teeth and held my tongue, and when Miss Albright demanded straight out to see what had been more important than her lesson, so help me, I acted, if not spoke, a lie. I fished out the notes I'd started earlier for her upcoming literary-analysis assignment and passed them over.

Miss Sadie looked disconcerted and said "Oh," and "I'm glad to see you've at least been giving some thought to your proper work."

I mumbled, "Yes, ma'am," took the papers back and

slid away. I could not, to save my soul, have shown her what I really had been doing, which was an essay for Mrs. Owens.

When I reached her classroom, the meeting had already started. I slipped into the seat Celinda'd saved, and Stella, on my other side, leaned across to mutter, "Look in the front row. What did I tell you?"

Mary Lou Hodge, wearing her sister Viney's peek-a-boo blouse.

I really did think she could have shown more sense that that, but I only murmured back, "It's a free country." I was feeling good because I had been made Feature Editor of the *Literary Magazine* for the balance of the year.

A date for a *Literary Magazine* editorial meeting was picked; the president asked for volunteers to work with the editors. Mary Lou's hand shot up before all others. "It looks like we'll have more than enough. The editors can confer and let you know who's needed," the president said, noting down names.

The Living Pictures Show was enthusiastically discussed, and the date, Friday, the twenty-fourth of January, was approved. "We'll need volunteers for that, too," the president announced.

Again, Mary Lou's hand was the first one up. Quick as a flash Stella, with uncharacteristic disregard for parliamentary procedure, called out, "I suggest the president appoint a General Chairman and leave the delegation of assignments to that person."

"All right with everybody? Then I appoint Stella Molloy. Any other business to be brought up? If not, I've got a lot of homework waiting. This meeting is adjourned."

I have no particular respect myself for parliamentary

41

formality, but it did occur to me some railroading was going on. It wasn't right, and somebody ought to have the gumption to point it out; but I pushed the thought away. I moved through the departing throng to Mrs. Owens and, before I could turn chicken, thrust my private essay at her. "Here." I moved off quickly then, but not before I'd seen the look of—relief? gladness?— that crossed Mrs. Owens's face. It was almost as if she'd been holding her breath waiting to see if I would come.

"Thank you," she said quietly, and I ran down the hall toward the cloakroom, singing a silly song beneath my breath.

Everyone else had already gone home, and the school had a spooky, deserted quality. No, not deserted. My heart sank as Mary Lou emerged out of the shadows just as I was pinning on my hat.

"I've got to talk to you," she said without preamble.

Oh, Lordy, I thought, she wants to volunteer for editorial staff, and I don't know what to do about it. "Can it wait till tomorrow? It's my turn to cook dinner this week, and I'm dreadful late."

"No, it can't. I can't wait another twenty-four hours without knowing. You're the only one can tell me— have you, have the Lathams heard anything at all about Doug?" A dull, unbecoming red rose in her cheeks. "I couldn't ask Kenneth. I've been so worried . . . and that story in the paper Sunday, it's just the kind of thing that could happen to that stupid fool . . . "

I stared at her. "You still love him, don't you?" I said slowly. "In spite of everything, you still—"

Mary Lou's face flamed. "You *kid*. What the hell do you know about loving somebody if you have to ask? Of course he's a loud-mouthed, cowardly, rotten . . . but

42

what's that got to do with—'' She stopped abruptly. "Oh, hell, I should have known better than try to get any help from you.'' She stormed out, leaving me to follow very slowly, feeling rather sick.

Mary Lou still cared what happened to Doug, despite all he'd hurt her, despite how she saw through him. That made me feel humble, it made me feel ashamed. It made me feel decidedly uncomfortable about having sat through the discussions of her at our tea parties and through the railroading at Browning Society, without having said a word.

My head was spinning; I wished I could talk with Kenneth, but I couldn't, not on this. I still didn't know what was right in the matter of Mary Lou Hodge and Browning Society's reputation. Maybe there were no clear-cut rights or wrongs. But I did know this: One couldn't pass judgement in the way Stella seemed to think you could, because what was involved were human beings, their feelings and their needs.

I resolved to write a note to Mary Lou, telling her what Ken had told me: that Doug had found a job and had sent home money to make up for what he stole. And I decided to write on Mary Lou's behalf to Ken, and try to find out, without giving anything away, whether he knew if Doug was still all right.

43

January

As JANUARY slogged along toward February, writing, Browning Society, and afternoon tea parties became the fixed constants in my life.

"Tish is intoxicated on something," Stella said wickedly. "It couldn't be all those letters going back and forth to Pennsylvania?"

I just grinned at her and looked mysterious and knowing. What I was high as a kite on was the sense of having found direction, of being able to write at last and know it would be read by somebody who would approve and understand. I couldn't talk about my writing yet to Stella, or to anyone but Kenneth and Celinda, and even with them I was shy, curiously reluctant to let them know how seriously I took it.

I didn't mind their seeing the "public produce," like the assembly skit and the narration for the Living Pictures Show. The former went over with a glorious bang, and resulted in a number of manuscripts being submitted for *Literary Magazine* consideration.

My correspondence with Ken was flourishing, too. And somewhere, as January's thaw turned to wind and ice, we stopped saying *if* Ken came back and started talking about *when*.

The Lathams hadn't had any further word from Doug, Ken wrote, and I relayed this message to Mary Lou. I couldn't ask again without Ken wondering why, and I certainly didn't want to raise alarm. "We'd better wait and see what happens," was what I said to Mary Lou. She just nodded, and if she was still worried, she didn't let it show; she appeared again at Young People's splendidly overdressed, and pushed herself to the forefront in school with what more and more people began considering a brazen nerve.

"She's volunteered three times to be in the pictures show," Stella groaned, settling herself for tea at our kitchen table one afternoon. "And twice she's asked if I've made up my mind yet who's doing what. Why doesn't Mrs. Owens take her off my hands?"

"Because Browning Society is supposed to be an organization of, by, and for the students," Larry pointed out with brotherly logic. "You can't have it both ways, you know, Miss Suffragette."

"At this point I wish I could," Stella retorted. "I wish I'd never agreed to take this stupid job." She laughed suddenly. "I should have asked Mary Lou if she'd pose as Hester Prynne in *The Scarlet Letter*. That would have fixed her."

Ben, who had risen to replenish the cookie plate,

45

turned around and scowled. "That wasn't particularly funny."

"Neither is Mary Lou's trying to be the leading light of the high school after all that's happened."

"You women make me sick," Ben said abruptly. "You could at least give the poor dumb kid a chance. If people hadn't always been expecting—"

He stopped, his face dark, and Stella took a good look at him and stayed shut up, too. I said hastily, "How *is* the Living Pictures Show coming?" It was only a week and a half away.

Stella looked relieved at the change of subject. "Fine, I think. That is, I've dragooned enough people for all the scenes we've planned. Anne's making posters to go up in the halls tomorrow. Now all," she accented with irony, "*all* we have to do is locate props and costumes, and probably have rehearsals every day next week."

"I'll help with costumes," Celinda volunteered, and Marnie and Jimmie were attracted at the thought of getting out of the house on week nights to attend rehearsals and offered to help with props.

"I wish I could do more," I said, "but I've got *Literary Magazine* material that has to be turned in to the printers the same day."

"You wrote the whole narration, and it's a good one," Stella responded generously. "You could read it for the show, yourself, if you have time."

I cannot say that the thought of appearing again onstage, especially reading my own words, displeased me. I wrote about it right away to Ken, who wrote back promptly that perhaps next year we could be on that stage again together.

I was writing a great many letters, most of them at

46

two or three A.M., a fact of which my parents fortunately were not aware. I was writing pieces for Mrs. Owens, too, almost every day, though she had not yet returned any to me. When I handed in three in a row she laughed and said, "Tish, stop rushing! Take your time and strive for quality."

"I'm not rushing, except to catch my thoughts down on paper before they fly away!"

Everyone was infected by some stimulation in the cold crisp air. Peter got himself jobs shoveling sidewalks and piled up money like a railroad baron. Mama was even more in the swing of business life and bustled around like a brisk brown bird. Pa was chafing at the bit, wanting to get back to the school himself. Ben was always vanishing to somewhere, though he had not yet designed to take us into his confidence.

As for Stella, she was stirring up a storm, running the Living Pictures Show like a general and loving every minute of it. By the Tuesday before it, she was snapping orders that were getting a lot of backs up but were also getting things done efficiently.

"Tish! Aren't you ever going to come to a rehearsal for the show? I *asked* if you were going to have the time," she said as we left school that day.

I could feel my hackles rising. "If you'd rather I didn't do it—"

"I didn't say that," Stella backed down hastily. "Let's invite ourselves to Celinda's for tea."

Celinda, who had reached home just before us, took one look and put the kettle on. "What happened?" she demanded, pushing a hassock in the direction of Stella's feet.

Stella threw herself down. "I think I've just inserted my foot in my big mouth, as Marnie would say."

47

"Would it help to be more specific?" Celinda asked, and Stella replied somberly, "Mary Lou Hodge."

"Oh, no," I exclaimed involuntarily, and Stella grimaced.

"Don't worry, I didn't say the things that should be said. She caught me unawares, and I lost my wits. Before I knew it, I heard myself asking her to be an usher Friday night." She looked at us and added defensively, "I know it's soft-headed, but in spite of everything, I can't help feeling sorry for her, somehow."

"I'm glad you did it," Celinda said slowly. "Even if maybe it wasn't the smartest thing to do."

"I'm pretty sure it wasn't," Stella said.

My head was starting to hurt. "Oh, let's not get into this again. What's done is done. I've got to get home, this is my week to cook." I went home, feeling like a coward, and found a letter waiting there for me from Ken.

That was not surprising; we wrote each other nearly every day. But this one was different. Doug *had* been the "D. Latham" we read about in that train accident.

"The sheriff who was taking an interest in him wrote to Mother. Doug didn't want us to know anything he was doing, as usual." I could almost hear the bitter weariness in Kenneth's voice. "He must have been up to something. Accidents don't just happen, not to Doug."

When I finished reading the brief letter, I knew I had to sit down and answer it right away, no matter how late dinner reached the table. Fortunately, nobody was at home, not even Pa who should have been; he'd been warned that falls on icy sidewalks would do his healing eyes no good at all. But I didn't stop to worry, other than to hope Peter had put enough ashes on the path. I got out the remains of Sunday's ham and some potatoes

48

and onions to cut up and fry, and then I just sat down at the table in the big silent kitchen, tore out a sheet of notebook paper, and wrote to Ken. I didn't say too much about the accident other than reminding him Doug had a way of landing on his feet. Most of the letter was painting a picture of next year, when Ken would be back here, when troubles would be over. I took infinite pains with it, knowing I was probably building a fool's paradise, knowing Ken needed that because it was all he had to hold to. The thought crossed my mind that perhaps this was what Mary Lou was doing, too.

I was just finishing when Ben walked in the back door and wanted to know why dinner wasn't ready yet.

"It will be. Where have you been?"

"Out. I saw a letter from your gentleman friend waiting for you when I came through earlier. It was about Doug and that train accident, wasn't it?"

I stared at him. "How did you know?"

"Because his writing on the envelope looked like hen's scratches instead of the usual copper plate." Without my asking, Ben sat down across from me and began peeling potatoes to be fried. "How bad is it, Tish? Dang all, Doug's my friend."

"You sound like Mary Lou." I laughed, rather shakily, and Ben nodded.

"I imagine she does feel the same. What *is* it about that rotter, anyway? He makes you hurt and hate till you wish one of you were dead—but you can't forget him, and you can't not care what happens."

I could not answer, and we sat in silence as the twilight turned to black outside the windows. Then Ben rose and slapped the potatoes in a cast-iron skillet on the stove, and as they snapped and sputtered I said in a low voice, "It's pretty bad. He was trying to—to jump

49

from one car to another when they had fallen into a ravine, I guess, and he hurt his leg. Ken thinks he was probably up to his old tricks, hopping freights."

"I guess that's one worry they won't have anymore, not after this. Where is he, did Ken say?"

"They don't know. Out West. That's another thing Doug's managed to keep from them. All they know is the sheriff's an ex-gunfighter whose name is Jones."

"I've been thinking I might ask Mr. Grimes to help me find him."

"Mr. Grimes!" I stared at Ben. "Is that where you've been vanishing to lately? Why didn't you say?"

"Because a fellow likes some privacy," Ben said coolly. "Mr. Grimes has a pal who works on the *Tribune*. I'll bet he'd know how I could locate Doug."

I felt like saying everyone was better off without Doug, but I couldn't. Ben read my mind. "Watching Unhappy Hodge trailing, or rather sailing, around makes me think that Doug could really use a friend."

"Friend," I said bitterly. "He doesn't even know what friendship means."

"Maybe," Ben said, "that's because he's never needed one before."

Mama came home and started getting worked up about everyone who was missing, particularly Pa. She cross-examined both of us, and Peter and Marnie too when they returned. "Think you could show a little concern! Dark already, slippery sidewalks, your father still getting over a delicate operation. Tarnation fool, should think he'd have more sense. Just a minute, young lady!" she snapped to Marnie who was taking off her coat. "You hustle down to Bronwyn's, collect the young ones, ask your sister if she knows where your father's gone."

"For pity's sake, Mama," Marnie said impatiently, "Pa's a grown man. He doesn't need a nursemaid."

The door opened while she was in mid-sentence, and we beheld Pa and our youngest siblings. "A point well taken, Evie. I've brought the youngsters."

"So I notice," Mama retorted. "Old fool. Wouldn't think of your own safety, might have considered the baby's. Could have fallen, broken both your necks."

Pa handed Katie to me and began unbuttoning his coat. "You may be Acting Principal, Mrs. Sterling," he said quietly, "but please don't let it go to your head when you're at home. I'm not one of your students or your children."

Mama looked at him and got very busy unwinding Katie out of her cocoon.

"Where were you off to, Pa?" Ben asked casually.

"Spent the afternoon with Sidney at his office. I tell you, it was good to get back to a business atmosphere. A man can get claustrophobia cooped up at home," Pa said firmly. "Starting next week, I'm going down to the school at least part of every day. Enough's enough."

I shot a glance at Mama, but she didn't say a word.

Ben, Marnie and I all went to the high school for the rehearsal of the Living Pictures that evening. The place was a cheerful madhouse. Mary Lou was there, helping paint scenery, which made me feel good somehow.

Ben looked at me. "You going to tell her what you heard from Ken?"

"I ought to. She wants to know. Oh, drat it, anyway, I hate to have to hand her the bad news. This is the first time I've seen her looking halfway happy."

Ben's eyes went from me to her, and back, with an unreadable expression. "Rats!" he said suddenly. "I'm Doug's friend. *I'll* tell her. Later."

Stella didn't look too pleased when she saw Ben in a tête-à-tête with Mary Lou, but I did not explain. First because I do have more sense than to get caught in the middle of the relationship between Ben and Stella. Second because, immediately after the conference, Mary Lou disappeared. Everyone else might have been relieved about that, but I was worried. I made a point of glancing, carefully casual, through our pile of wraps, and that conspicuous bright plaid coat was gone.

It bothered me, the thought of Mary Lou walking home alone at night. There wasn't much I could do about it, though. Then it occurred to me that if Ben could consult Mr. Grimes about Doug Latham, I could talk about Mary Lou to Mrs. Owens.

I found her surrounded by a knot of people, all demanding instant answers to their problems. She looked tired. "Tish, if you've come to ask about your work, I'm sorry. Between this project and the magazine, on top of regular lessons, I've been pressed for time."

"I know. It's not that." I edged her away from the others and outlined the Hodge situation briefly. "I'm worried about it. She—well, you know how reckless she can be when she gets wound up."

"Yes, I do." Mrs. Owens's shoulders sagged. "I'll get the janitor to unlock the office so I can telephone her home." She went off, and I waited until she had come back, shrugging wryly. "I spoke to her father. They're a strange family; I don't think he appreciated my interfering, but anyway, he's going to go out and meet her."

The rehearsal, while certainly not brilliant, definitely showed promise of a good entertainment, and I basked in compliments on both my narrative script and its delivery. But I found myself more concerned about Mrs. Owens's reaction to the material I'd given her. This work tonight was all on the surface, though I had endeavored to do it carefully and well. But the other was real, the other mattered. Somewhere inside of me, as the days had gone by without acknowledgement, butterflies had started fluttering.

Mrs. Owens called me into her classroom the next afternoon. "I felt so bad about having kept you waiting that I went home last night and read all your papers through three times, carefully. I wanted to do that, so I could get beyond the emotional spell they conjure and see the way you put the bricks together."

She hesitated. "You're not going to like this, Tish," she said at last, "but Miss Albright's right. You do need to learn structure."

"I thought," I heard my own voice saying carefully, "you thought that I could write."

"I know you *are* a writer. That's a different thing. But there is more to being a professional writer than being able to evoke a mood and to put words on paper beautifully. I take it that what you wanted, when you asked me to help you, was to learn to write professionally?"

For a moment, I almost hated her. "You know I did," I said in that same noncommital, Stella-like voice.

"Then you have to take the time to learn the discipline of your craft. Just as a musician, however gifted, has to devote time to theory and fingering and scales." Mrs. Owens opened her desk drawer and took out a detailed syllabus. "I have worked out a list of specific assignments for you. Each is for a definite purpose, which I have noted. Each has specific requirements of slanting, form, and length. I want you to force yourself to work within them. It won't be easy, but just now

53

this is the best sort of training you could possibly have."

"Are you saying the . . . other things I gave you aren't any good?"

Mrs. Owens regarded me with an unreadable expression. " 'Good' is not the point; that's what I've been saying. They have magic, as you very well know; they have heart and soul. What they do not have is recognizable literary form. What do you really want, Tish; to improve your writing or just to be complimented on what's already there?"

I picked up the syllabus and my rejected papers. "I'll have the first assignment in on Friday," I said rigidly, and left.

I went over to Celinda's, and Stella was there. I couldn't talk in front of her, I wasn't sure that I could talk at all, but I needed Celinda's comforting presence. She had made tea, and Stella was talking a mile a minute about all the latest ramifications of the Living Pictures Show. At last Stella rose to go, and I contrived to linger. Celinda shut the door on Stella's departing curiosity and turned to me with a tender look.

"What's the matter? Something is, I know, but I didn't think I ought to ask in front of Stel."

I handed her the pages Mrs. Owens had scorned. "Read these, will you?" I waited, hands clasped tightly, as she did so. "What do you think?"

"They're wonderful," Celinda said. "You know I think everything you write is wonderful. But what are they for?"

"For?"

"You're too busy to be putting words together just for the sake of making beautiful sentences."

There was an uncomfortable echo there of something

Mrs. Owens had said. "They're not for anything. I just felt like writing them, and I wanted an opinion."

Celinda looked at me and came over to put her two hands on my shoulders. "Someday I'm going to be able to say, 'Letitia Sterling? Oh, yes, I read her things before anyone else had ever heard of them.' I'll be proud of you then, and I'm proud of you now." She hugged me hard. "You are a writer, and don't you ever doubt it."

But a writer wasn't a real writer until his work was read, not just by himself and his near and dear, but by the world to whom he had things that he must say.

I went home, gritted my teeth, and sat down and wrote the assignment Mrs. Owens wanted. It wasn't easy; I was irritated and discouraged, but I kept at it doggedly. I was chewing it over in my head when we left to go to school for that night's rehearsal, and while there I snapped at a couple of people who inquired whether my head was in the clouds or in Pennsylvania. When I got home, I was still carrying on my inner argument with Mrs. Owens, and I hadn't even begun the homework due next day to Sourpuss Sadie and Mr. Moore. It was a good thing my parents didn't notice that light was escaping through the crack beneath my door till long past three.

I wound up next morning with a splitting headache, which did not exactly make for good relations all around, especially since Ben was gloomy. He'd tried to get in touch with Mr. Grimes about Doug, he told me privately, and had had no answer.

"It's enough to drive a fellow wild, to finally drive yourself into taking an important step you've wrestled with and have it fizzle out."

I knew exactly how he felt.

55

"I don't suppose you've heard anything more from Kenneth?" Ben said with wan hope, and I shook my head.

"He's probably only today getting the letter I wrote to him."

I did hope that in that letter, at least, I had succeeded in saying what I meant to say.

In school when I had a chance I reread the exercise paper I had labored over for Mrs. Owens, and to my jaundiced eye it was passionless, unemotional, it was dead. I tried to tell you, Mrs. O., I thought; when I stick to prescribed form and structure, the magic dies. Without inspiration, there can be no art, and this . . . slaving . . . kills any magic that does come.

That blasted argument in my head—with myself, with Mrs. Owens, I didn't know whom—kept dogging me. Stella took my head off that afternoon because I was short with her when she requested an alteration in my narration. And later when we were putting a cake together for Katie's first birthday celebration at dinnertime, Marnie asked me point-blank what was going on.

"Did you and Kenneth have a fight or something? The last couple of weeks you went around grinning like a Cheshire cat, and all of a sudden you've done a hundred-and-eighty degree turn."

"I'm sorry. I didn't mean to burden anyone with my black moods."

"Oh, you haven't," Marnie said frankly. "Maybe that's the trouble. "If you want to let off steam, or anything, I'm here."

But I couldn't tell her, or anyone, what I was feeling, not even Kenneth, not even Mrs. Owens.

Through the birthday dinner, which Bron's household, Aunt Kate and Miss Sadie all attended, and afterwards when I lay awake in bed, that battle in my head went on. I lit the lamp and again reread the assignment. And as I read, I began to see her point. Yet, though I might be proud of the labor I had invested in it, I wasn't proud of how it had turned out, not by half. I'll be danged if I'm going to turn something in with the magic absent, I thought on Friday, and instead of listening to the announcement for the Living Pictures Show being made in the Assembly, I found my mind drifting off on how I would have written that assignment if I hadn't been obliged to follow rules.

It started happening; the magic started coming back, swallowing me into the half-consciousness of a waking dream. I couldn't lose—what had Ken once called it?— the mustard seed of magic. I was more afraid of the bleakness of life without it than I was of what Miss Sadie would say if she caught me doing private writing in my notebook instead of listening to her English class.

I wrote the whole blamed composition over, my way; then I skipped lunch entirely, holed away in the girls' cloakroom, and spent the whole noon hour dovetailing the two versions together into one composite whole. Now, I thought at last, hungry but content, maybe both Mrs. Owens and I can be satisfied.

I drifted through the rest of the school day feeling drained but mellow, laid the completed work on Mrs. Owens's desk at three, together with the final editorial work I'd done on *Literary Magazine*, and went home to restore myself with bread-butter-and-sugar and a pot of tea.

The whole family was going to the Living Pictures Show that night, including Pa who'd put his foot down and flatly refused to be treated like a semi-invalid any longer. "I'm going back to work the beginning of the week. Talked to Doc Tuttle, and he didn't say no; so Evie, you might as well start getting used to the idea. Sidney says he'll drive me back and forth, so you needn't start your song and dance about slippery walks."

"*Us*," Mama said. "He'll drive the two of us. Not going to stop going down, turn the whole load back on you straight off, know how you'll overdo."

"All right, us," Pa said. "Feel like a courting couple again, won't we, the two of us setting off together."

Mama snorted, but her eyes were twinkling.

Sidney also drove the family to the Living Pictures Show, with Bron staying home to mind the infants so Mama could hear me deliver the narration that I'd written. Even Missie was allowed to stay up and attend, since the Living Pictures Show was planned to be a fairly early evening.

The Living Pictures were an artistic success and, having been carefully chosen, were innocuous enough for the whole neighborhood to approve. But the biggest show of the evening, and decidedly controversial, was Mary Lou Hodge, who showed up to usher wearing an overelaborate pompadour and her sister Viney's notorious peek-a-boo blouse.

Mrs. Owens was backstage, engrossed in a multitude of details, when Mary Lou unveiled this tawdry splendor, which probably explains why the situation wasn't dealt with tactfully there and then. The first I heard of it was when Stella seized me in the wings, a few seconds before the lights went down.

"Did you see her? She looks like something off a burlesque poster. I just caught a glimpse through the curtain crack, and what's more Miss Albright and your aunt are staring at her with judgement in their eyes.''

"Wouldn't you think she'd have had more sense? And why didn't the president make her go home and change? He's right out there taking tickets at the door.''

"He's male,'' Stella said scathingly. "He either didn't notice her clothes, or he noticed too much and didn't use his head. But Miss Sadie's head's working, I'll bet you anything.''

The house lights went out, to the accompaniment of applause and stamping feet. There were the usual cat-calls and silly giggles; then the footlights went up and Stella stepped out, flushed and self-possessed, to welcome the audience and introduce the program.

I read my narration, and it and I were well received. So was the program; there was so much applause we were obliged to reopen the curtains to encore several popular scenes. Mrs. Owens was pleased, congratulating everyone on the hard work done, announcing we'd taken in enough money to guarantee *Literary Magazine* printing bills for the balance of the year. I gathered from her manner that nobody'd gossiped to her yet about Mary Lou's attire; I hoped the necessity would not arise.

It was an empty hope. We all went back to Bron's for hot chocolate and dessert, and Miss Sadie and Aunt Kate raced each other to see who'd be the first to explode with righteous wrath.

"Girl obviously hasn't learned a thing . . . ''

" . . . knew there would be trouble if the hussy were allowed . . . ''

" . . . undesireable influence . . .

" . . . moral leaders; have a Christian duty to reprimand . . . '' And on, and on.

I was sick to death of the whole subject of Mary Lou Hodge.

I didn't see any of the crowd on Saturday; the reality of approaching exams had hit. Even Marnie and Ben were studying, and I retreated to my bedroom window-seat with a couple of apples and my history textbook. In midmorning Marnie knocked and entered. "Mailman came. I thought you'd want this right away." She handed me an envelope in Kenneth's writing.

I tore it open so avidly I didn't even notice that she lingered. "Is anything wrong with Ken?" she said at last.

"What? Oh, no. Except, of course, he's worried about Doug."

"I only asked on account of the queer way you've been acting. All right, I'm not going to pry. But I do think it'd be easier on you, as well as everyone else, if you didn't try to live in six separate worlds at once."

She vanished, leaving me staring at Kenneth's letter in some confusion. Separate worlds. That was what I was creating, wasn't it? Kenneth, my writing, home and school. It certainly wasn't what I'd set out to do. But it's necessary, a voice within me said. Kenneth needs the private world of him-and-me. I need a world of my own in which to write, unimpeded by discouragements and distractions. Yet that other voice in my head reminded me, you want to write about reality, remember? To portray the real world of thoughts and feelings, to influence it, to help it. And that's not possible in an ivory tower.

I wound up with another splitting headache and the uneasy feeling that in trying to keep my separate worlds from colliding, I wasn't being my real self in any of them.

February

ON MONDAY, the twenty-seventh of January, exams and a heavy snowstorm began together. Mama was having conniptions because Pa still insisted on going down to the secretarial school. "Land sakes, Evie," he finally exploded, "anybody'd think by now you'd be glad to have me going back to work, take the load off you! Not an old man, not going to settle for doing nothing the rest of my born days!"

Mama pressed her lips together and by a heroic effort forebore a sermon. They whirled off toward downtown in Sidney Albright's stylish cutter, and we set out through snowdrifts in the opposite direction.

There was one fortunate by-product of those loathed exams—much less gossip about Mary Lou than I'd expected. Everyone's time and minds were occupied by weightier matters.

By the end of the day, I was exhausted. I needed restoring, and I didn't mean the too-easy narcotic of tea and gossip with the girls.

I went, without having consciously thought about it, to Mrs. Owens's room. The door was closed, but I peered in through the glass. Mrs. Owens was sitting at her desk, her dark head bent across a pile of papers. She looked tired; there were circles underneath her eyes. I felt, unaccountably, like an intruder and rather lonely, and I was about to tiptoe off when she looked up, caught my glance and smiled.

"Tish, hello. I thought you might be by." She pushed her work aside as I opened the door and hesitated on the threshold. "Have your ears been ringing? There have been some very nice comments about your work on the show last Friday." She didn't mention any comments about Mary Lou Hodge, and I did not ask. "Come in and stay awhile, if you have time."

"Aren't you too busy?"

Mrs. Owens shook her head. "I only gave one exam today, and it can wait. Everything's quiet this afternoon, which is good. It will give us a chance to have a private talk."

Something inside me fell with a hollow thud.

"You didn't like that paper I wrote for you," I said flatly.

Mrs. Owens gave me a level look. "Did *you?*"

It is terribly disconcerting to have one's own questions twisted around on one, with no clue to the other person's thoughts. All at once I no longer felt convinced I was pleased with that paper, but I was sure of one thing, I liked it much better than I had before I'd tampered with it to insert some magic.

"I have a feeling," Mrs. Owens said, "that I've been reading two separate papers, put together. Rather like what Stella was doing when she was trying to play Nora in *A Doll's House* two ways, hers and mine."

I didn't answer. I didn't have to, and she knew it.

Mrs. Owens took out the paper, and it was as splashed with red ink as anything Sadie Albright had ever handed back.

"I did try," I said defensively. "I really did, and it went bad on me, like when you overmix egg whites into cake batter and it all goes flat. So I tried to do what you wanted me to and still have the magic in."

"And what you got, if you want to continue the cooking metaphor, is what happens when you're not careful adding eggs to a hot sauce," Mrs. Owens said drily. "The whole thing curdles. Separates into two incompatible mixtures that will not blend."

"But I tried to—"

Mrs. Owens put up her hand. "Tish, wait, please. Don't bother explaining how hard you tried, or what you tried, because I know. Just sit and read the paper and my comments carefully."

For a long time there was no sound in the room but the ticking of the clock. When I looked up at last, I knew to my shame that tears were spilling.

"I don't understand. I really don't. I've read it over three times carefully, and I just get more confused. You say, 'structure,' and I tried to follow the structure you gave me to the letter—"

"—till you got wrapped up in magic-making and forgot," Mrs. Owens interposed.

"There's got to be magic! Otherwise the writing's dead. You told me once that was the real gift I had, not to ever lose it, the ability to evoke mood and emotion, to make others feel. Well, when I try to follow rigid form rather than inspiration, I *do* lose it. I get self-conscious. The magic goes—"

"It won't, in time."

Mrs. Owens's matter-of-fact assurance was like an impenetrable facade. "You don't understand—I don't know what you want. Here you say 'excellent, vivid description,' and on the next page, 'purple, overwritten,' when I'm practically doing the exact same thing. You say 'no content, just emotional bathos,' when even reading my own words here almost tears my heart out." I stared at her across the enormous gulf of two rows of desks. "Why did you tell me I had the gift of writing if you're going to tear down the only parts of it I know I can do well?"

When Mrs. Owens spoke, it was with what seemed absolute irrelevance. "Tish, have you ever seen colored pictures of buildings in Shakespeare's country, in the Cotswolds?"

I nodded, not looking in her direction.

"I was there once," Mrs. Owens said. Her voice took on an odd tone, as if she was stepping back through time. "There's magic there, a very special magic. The stones themselves are so filled with light they almost seem alive. They have a—a power of evocation. Just to look at them, lying in a pile, is to be moved. But the buildings made from them, those buildings that have endured for seven hundred years, they have an even greater power and a strength. And what is more, they serve a purpose. Those unknown artisans who built them created living art because they understood the stones, they worked with the grain of them, not against it. It was their skill, the underlying order that the material itself dictated but which those men put together with thought and sweat and mortar, that's what made homes and churches for people out of what otherwise would have remained just a pile of stones. Do you understand what I am saying?"

"No," I said stubbornly. "No, I don't." Outside the window, snow fell silently through the purpling sky.

"Your words have magic, just like those stones do," Mrs. Owens said. "But unless you learn to understand underlying structure, unless you learn to use the tools and mortar of your craft, you're going to end up with nothing but a pile of stones." She picked up the detested paper I had pushed away. "I *could* have written on this, 'beautiful description.' That's probably what I would have done, had you submitted this as an essay in a sophomore English class. But I paid you the respect of thinking you were after higher things. That's all this is, Tish, a good high school English paper. It's not an essay, it is not a story. It communicates emotion, yes, but that is all. And that, in the professional marketplace, makes it melodrama. If you want to be *read,* you have to foreswear your addiction to magic until you are a master. You have to practice with dull grey stone, as the old apprentices did. Then, when the moment for the magic comes, it will return. That I promise you."

There was so much suppressed passion in her voice that it would have astounded me if I had not been so shaken. Even while my eyes stared at her numbly, she added the final, killing stroke. "You did know you were opening Pandora's box when you started all this, Tish. You are not so innocent. In writing, there is no hiding nor avoiding embarrassment or pain."

It hurt; oh, it hurt, and she had meant it to. And in my pain, in my embarrassment and humiliation, I lashed back with the first, the most brutal weapon that came into my mind.

"You're talking to me about professional writing standards. If you're so sure of them, how come *you're* not a writer, instead of just teaching writing to kids in school?"

I didn't wait to see the look upon her face. My eyes were blinded, and I was running out of there, down the hall, stumbling and choking. I grabbed my coat and hat from the empty cloak room and blundered down the stairs, out into the steadily falling snow.

I needed someone, I needed not to be alone. I needed Kenneth, but Kenneth wasn't there, and even Celinda's maternal, too-anxious comforting would not help. The only place I could think to go was to Bronwyn's.

I could hardly see straight as I fumbled through the drifts. The snow stung my face and mingled with my tears. At least, if I could get myself under control before I reached Bron's door, I would be spared humiliating explanations of wet eyes. I plodded doggedly up streets deserted except for the occasional sleigh with its lonely bells. Three more houses, two; the lights of the Albright windows reached out to me through the gathering dark.

I pushed the gate open and dragged myself up the steps, opened the front door and went in without waiting for an answer, calling, "Bron?"

"Come on in."

It wasn't Bron's voice that answered. It was Junius, sprawled out comfortably before the parlor fire, rocking the baby's cradle with one big toe as he softly strummed the strings of his guitar.

66

I put my brakes on, willing my voice calm. "Isn't Bronwyn here?"

"She wanted to go to Ladies' Aid; she got wind from Aunt Sadie that there's a catfight brewing. So I said I'd watch the infants." Junius was shrewder than my sister would have been. "Which were you looking for, a corner to hide in or a place to talk?"

"A corner to hide, I think."

He waved his arm casually. "Help yourself."

I had no intention whatever of staying, but I found myself shedding my hat and coat. "Better take your shoes off, too," Junius said, not looking up from the string that he was tuning. The Oriental carpet was warm with heat from the registers, and my sister Katie was crawling about happily. She pulled herself up with the aid of the Morris chair, wavered a moment, and toppled over with a startled grunt. I dropped down beside her, burying my face in her curls.

Junius left the room and presently came back to set a cup of steaming coffee wordlessly beside me. He makes good coffee. I sipped it silently, as he folded himself up before the fire again and began to play a complicated fugue. Katie, having crawled into my lap, settled herself like a puppy and went to sleep. A log cracked and separated, sending up a shower of sparks.

"Junius," I said at last, "you can be very comforting."

"Glad to know I'm good for something."

"Don't start that. Not today. I'm in the same mood myself."

Junius grinned. "What's the matter, somebody cut you down to midget size? It wasn't by any chance my aunt?"

"From her it wouldn't have been so unexpected. As it

was—I just don't like myself very much right now."

"Other folks do. That should count for something."

"What counts," I said carefully, "is whether particular people like particular things I do."

"Then you don't really mean what they think of *you* at all."

"What I do *is* me."

"You mean your writing?" Junius asked calmly.

I stared at him. "How did you—?"

He shrugged. "Everyone knows you write. I don't mean that script for the Browning Society show. Real things, like that story in *Literary Magazine* last month about the selling of your grandfather's farm. I noticed you never talk about them, but you understand how I feel about my music, so I figured. . . . Is that what happened? Did somebody who matters not appreciate?"

"You couldn't be more right," I said grimly.

"Then you can see why I don't want to play in public."

"It makes a private world for you, doesn't it?" I said slowly. "The music."

He nodded. "And if somebody tramps on it with big flat feet . . . something's ruined."

"The sanctuary's gone. I know. I know." I was silent for a moment. "That's what writing's been for me, a private place. But lately something's been changing in me. *I've* been changing. I need to open that place up, use writing as a means to share. . . . Only when I try, it doesn't seem to work."

"It did in that story. Lots of people said so."

"That story was a stroke of luck," I said bitterly. "I didn't *try* to write it, it wrote itself, and it was sheer chance it went together right, because apparently I don't know the proper form."

"You could learn," Junius said; and I came right back, "You could study music, too, but I don't catch you willingly submitting to the knife."

Junius, attempting a complicated run of notes, hit a false one, stopped, tried and again, failed, and set the guitar away.

"Please don't stop."

His face closed. "I don't like making a fool of myself in public, any more than you."

"*I'm* not public. No one could expect you to know everything straight off. How can you ever learn unless you try? Just because you make mistakes in the process, nobody's going to think less of you, or of your gift—and you do have one, false notes or no." I stopped abruptly.

Junius looked at me. "Does the shoe pinch?"

"I have a habit," I said ruefully, "of learning the most when I hear my big mouth preaching to someone else."

As I carried Katie home through the cold and dark, I decided to go on trying to write for Mrs. Owens. And I wasn't going to speak to her of what had passed between us—not now, perhaps not ever. Call it cowardice, call it weakness, I knew that the only way I could go on encountering Mrs. Owens was to act as if today had never been.

I needed to confess my sins to someone, though, and Kenneth was the only one of whose judgement I was not afraid. "I did a terrible thing today," I wrote that night, and then it all spilled out. I ended up by enclosing the red-inked papers Mrs. Owens had handed back. Then I closed my mind resolutely to the temptation of my journal and devoted the rest of the evening to the next day's math exam.

The snow continued all that night, and by morning a harsh wind was whipping up drifts that were shoulder-high. Pa and Mama had another argument about who was going to the school. "You ought to stay home yourself in this weather," Pa said bluntly. "Then we wouldn't have to be taking a child that age out in this storm to be watched by someone else."

Mama's eyes narrowed. "You by any chance been listening to your sister Kate make comments 'bout my not taking proper care of my own child? Baby a year old now, real Sterling, healthy little savage, never believed in coddling children, encourages sickliness."

"I never thought you believed in coddling perfectly healthy adults, either."

Mama snorted. "Think you'd appreciate my concern. Not to mention work I've been doing."

"I do. It's far more than I ever wanted you to have to—"

"Hardest job," Mama said point-blank, "is riding herd on *you*. Saw you yesterday, poring over students' papers, rubbing your eyes. *And* going over all the entries in the ledger. All those figures, harsh white paper, too much strain. What were you thinking of, anyway? Got no need."

"I was trying," Pa said with dignity, "to put the records back in proper order."

"*Are* in order. Better than when I found 'em. Spent two weeks getting them in shape."

"*Pa,*" Marnie said urgently, "Sidney's waiting in the cutter, and it's cold out there."

That got them moving, but Marnie and I exchanged troubled glances. "I don't think," Marnie said as we set out toward school, "they're having any picnic down there, the two of them."

"It won't be for long. Pa's itching to take over at the school again, and Mama'll be back home."

"Mama," Marnie said, "has had a taste of Aunt Kate's Liberated Womanhood. You think she's going to be happy to give it up and go back to housework, which she's always hated?"

We looked at each other uneasily. "Remember what it was like last year, when they weren't speaking for a while," I said, and we all shuddered.

I was so busy following this new train of thought that I forgot to be worried about the math exam, and I didn't even think of Mrs. Owens until I saw her coming down the hall. Then I ducked into the nearest classroom until she'd passed. It wasn't planned, I just wasn't ready to face her, or to start on her next assignment.

It was Marnie's turn to cook this week, but nonetheless I went straight home from school and made a pecan pie. Something within us told us both that a splendid dinner would be a good idea.

I knew, as soon as Pa and Mama entered, that something had been going on. They weren't fighting, but Mama's chin was in the air, and Pa looked strained. I saw what Mama meant, too, about the way he rubbed his eyes. We didn't say anything, nor did Mama till Pa refused a second piece of pie and said he thought he'd go lie down.

"Eyes hurting, aren't they?" she snapped in that gruff way she uses to mask concern. "Could have told you. Serves you right, too, using them all that time, undoing all the work I'd done."

"It *was* necessary," Pa said patiently. "I had to get the books back in order before any more entries were made in them wrong."

"Weren't wrong. Spend two weeks working late,

getting them into a respectable order."

Pa took a deep breath, as though trying to hold onto his calm. "I'm sorry, Evie. I chose my word unwisely. I appreciate you had put them in a kind of order, you can't be blamed for not knowing the system I'd devised."

"Shorthand genius, not a bookkeeper," said my mother flatly. "We're losing the discounts for prompt payment half the time, 'cause you didn't notice."

"We'd better get started on the dishes," I said hastily. "Peter, you come dry. Pa, shall I take you some more coffee in your study?"

That ended that, at least, but I had an uncomfortable feeling there was more to come.

Everything hung in abeyance the balance of the week. Snow fell intermittently, and Peter the entrepreneur continued adding shoveling money to his bank every afternoon. We studied for exams, and took them. I had tea with Bron and heard how she had succeeded in heading off a discussion of Mary Lou Hodge's latest indiscretion by the Ladies' Aid. I continued avoiding Mrs. Owens in the corridors of school. But none of this seemed as real, as urgent, as it would once the pressures of exams were over.

And I still hadn't written the next assignment for Mrs. Owens.

On Thursday afternoon I received a bulky epistle in the mail from Ken. "I think I can see what Mrs. Owens means," Kenneth said. "So could you, probably, if it weren't part of your blood and bone. For one thing, where she's marked 'purple passages' and 'overwritten,' it's generally where you've been repeating words or patterns, or else where you've described the same thing three separate ways. You know how you always talk about your mother's 'Lecture #3481' and how you don't listen because you've heard it all before.''

I had the grace to grin at that.

"What you write, Tish, is so beautiful, but it's—I don't know, like pieces of a story, character study or description of the emotion of a given moment, not a story itself.''

I read my papers again, and I could see exactly what he meant. I could have kicked myself for not having done so in the first place. "But nobody told me,'' the defensive voice within me said. And the other voice, the one that had spoken to Junius about his music, answered, "Of course not. That's the point. No one expects you to know everything already, no one but you.''

I sat down with my writing tablet in my room that night and I thought, "All right. This time I'm going to do precisely what I'm told. I'll think of it as practicing scales, not writing, and I'll swallow the bitter pill.''

It was funny, once I approached what I was doing as a practice drill, or a game, the way Pa'd taught me to tackle math, it went a lot faster and less painfully. When I was finished, I made two copies, one for Mrs. Owens, one for Ken. Then, flushed with the virtue of self-discipline, I went at the research report for Sadie Albright I'd been putting off the whole past week. By this time it was pretty late and I was exhausted, but too wide-awake for sleep. I put my robe on, opened my bedroom door cautiously, and descended into the chilly darkness of the lower floor.

One of the advantages of Mama's going to business is that she's too tired to hear me when I prowl around at night. I found some leftover gingerbread and made a pot of tea, and was settling myself for this collation when the kitchen door opened and Pa wandered in.

73

"I thought I heard sounds of life. So you're awake, too, daughter?"

Pa hadn't even been to bed, but he looked as though he should have been. His eyes were sore. But I decided he wouldn't appreciate any comments on that subject. I got out another cup and saucer and poured him tea, and he sat down across from me, regarding me quizzically. "What have you been up to? Last minute studying for exam?"

"Last minute composition for Miss Albright. I deserve a hundred percent for effort, but she probably won't give me more than seventy-five."

"I don't know," Pa said mildly. "Seems to me you've been doing some pretty good writing lately. That program you put together for Browning Society was just right, very clever and entertaining."

"Oh, that!"

"It served the purpose it was aimed for, and very well, too. And then there was that story about the farm, in the *Literary Magazine*. I was very proud of that, Tish, for many reasons."

I couldn't speak; I felt tears gathering in my eyes.

"What's the matter?" Pa asked, "Sadie A. doesn't appreciate your literary efforts?"

"What do you think?"

"She's a good woman," Pa said judiciously, "but she's never been precisely what I'd call sensitive or perceptive. Kind of clumsy-footed, with the best intentions in the world. Look at the damage she did to that boy she brought up, though she'll never see it." Pa eyed me shrewdly. "Writing's come to mean a lot to you, hasn't it? Then let me give you a piece of good advice. Don't let the Sadie Albrights of this world, or anyone else, get you discouraged. Listen to their criticism, sure,

74

and learn from it, the way a professional would do. The professional keeps on going because something in him won't let him stop, and he learns the tricks of the trade because communication's just as important as self-expression.''

Why is it that sometimes every voice one hears sings the same tune?

"I've been proud of something else," Pa said, pouring us both more tea. "The way you young ones took hold around here while I was laid up. It will be easier soon, once your Ma's back home again. Then maybe you won't have to be doing homework in the middle of the night."

"Maybe Mama's one of those people you were talking about," I said daringly. "She may keep going because something inside her won't let her stop."

"I hope not, Tish. I certainly hope not. She's worked hard enough already, and she shouldn't have to."

"She really does enjoy it, Pa, you know."

"Yes, I can see that." Pa sounded discouraged. He looked at me, smiling wryly. "I tell you, sometimes it's not easy living in the twentieth century."

I left one copy of my composition exercise on Mrs. Owens's desk next day, and I put the other in the mail to Ken. In the future, I resolved, I was going to do those assignments early enough to send them to him for comments before submission. I took my last exam, and turned the research paper in to Sadie Albright. Then exams and January both were over. We celebrated at the Young People's get-together at Albrights' house that night.

These festivities also were in honor of Larry's shaking the dust of high school off his feet forevermore. He would be publicly graduated at commencement exercises in early June, but as of Monday morning he would be a full-fledged student at Columbia. He was, characteristically, eager to get started; but the look in Celinda's eyes told me how much she longed to hold him back.

There were two little pockets of false gaiety at Bronwyn's house that night; one was Celinda, and the other was Mary Lou. Oh, she was as raucous as she ever was; but all at once, as if we both were pulled by something we could not prevent, our eyes met, and I knew hers were asking whether I'd heard anything more of Doug. I shook my head, and the next day I sought out Ben in the attic where we could talk alone.

"Did you ever talk to Mr. Grimes the way you wanted?"

"Uh-huh." Ben tossed me an apple from the basket by his side. "If there's any way to locate Doug, he'll do it. I'm glad you pushed me into talking to him about it. Even if we never find Doug, it's been worthwhile, just getting to know Philip better."

"*Philip?*"

Ben shrugged. "He told me to call him that. We don't feel like teacher and student any more. He's . . . he's been a big help, Tish. With lots of things. I needed somebody. I've got to think about the future. That was Doug's trouble. He never did. But what can I do? Ma keeps talking about Harvard, but I know there's not enough money. Philip had me apply for a scholarship. I didn't dare tell Pa, or even ask him about it. He's so touchy these days."

I came away with an emptiness that was half loneliness, half envy. I knew exactly what he meant, and what he felt, because for a moment in time Mrs. Owens and I had been taking steps toward one another on that

76

same narrow bridge. Now I was avoiding Mrs. Owens, and I was doing it deliberately. I could not write for her and also talk to her.

Kenneth knew about it, via letters. Junius knew, because I formed the habit of stopping by to listen to him practice on Monday afternoons when Bron was off to Ladies' Aid. There was a kind of comfort in being orphans from the critical storm together, in knowing that we didn't need to talk.

Celinda could tell something was going on within me, but she didn't ask, and I felt like a heel because I couldn't tell her. I tried to make it up by being around when she needed a listening ear, or just companionship, for Celinda, too, finds it difficult to speak her different fears, and she felt lost without Larry and afraid of losing him.

In school, at Young People's, with the family, I was not exactly endearing myself with everyone. I ticked my failings off in my journal one night when I was filled with an overpowering necessity to explode. Flippancy; forgetfulness; tiredness; busy-ness. Inability to concentrate—that was the one that really riled Miss Sadie. Feeling lonely even when I was with a crowd of friends. Getting mad at Mrs. Owens for having confronted me with a mirror and a reflection I did not want to see.

Mrs. Owens. I could avoid her physical presence, but I couldn't get her out of my thoughts. I wrote the assignments she'd given me, and sent them first to Ken, and then with his perceptive comments to guide me revised them and left them on her desk when I knew she would not be there.

I knew I wouldn't be able to keep this up forever, and I dreaded the inevitable confrontation. Another deadline for *Literary Magazine* was coming due, the end of February, but I managed to make sure others were always present when I had to appear for editorial conferences. It was at Browning Society meeting, toward the end of February, that Mrs. Owens did finally catch up with me.

"Tish, it's been so long since I've seen you. I've looked for you often, lately, but you've never been around."

I marveled that her voice could be so equable, as if nothing in the world was wrong. "I've been very busy."

"But you've kept up with your work. I'm very glad of that."

She wasn't referring to my schoolwork.

"I have some papers to return to you. I'd really like to talk to you about them. Can you come tomorrow?"

I felt caught. "I . . . don't know. I'll see. Celinda's leaving, and I promised I would walk her home." I dashed off, not even waiting to say good-bye.

The next afternoon, as soon as the three o'clock bell rang, I dashed out of the school building, and made a beeline straight to Bron's. I spent a couple of hours ostensibly listening to Junius play, but what I was really seeing and hearing was Mrs. Owens.

The next day, as I was trying to leave quickly also, Ben's voice hailed me. "I'm glad I caught you." He pulled me hastily into an empty classroom as I stared at him.

"What's the matter?"

"I think we've finally got a lead on Doug. I'm catching the trolley to meet Phil Grimes at Columbia, and he's taking me to meet that friend of his at the *Tribune*. Philip says he's got some stuff for me to look over. Tish, I don't know how late I'll be, so keep Mama from getting worked up about it, will you? And don't, for

Pete's sake, tell her what I'm up to. You know how she feels about Doug Latham!"

He vanished, and I emerged into the hall to find Mrs. Owens.

I glanced frantically to the right and to the left, but there was no help in sight. I could only stand there in the deserted corridor as she came toward me, seeming to grow in stature as she approached.

"I waited for you yesterday, but you did not come."

"I know." I couldn't move.

"You have been deliberately avoiding me, Tish, haven't you?"

I could not speak the truth, and to lie or evade would have been folly.

"Your papers will be on my desk, in a folder with your name on it, any time you want them. *If* you want them. You can put others there, too, when and if you want." Her mouth twisted. "Call it Pandora's Box."

She went away, and after minutes that seemed like hours, I went too. I left the school building feeling physically weak.

It was my turn to cook dinner, and I spent the afternoon being very busy in the kitchen, trying not to think. I was basting loin of pork with cider when the back door opened and Aunt Kate stalked in. "Your Pa at home?"

"No, ma'am. He's at the school."

"Thought he was coming home early. Stopped by the school on my way home from Wanamaker's two hours ago, and he was thinking of it. His eyes looked like burned-out holes in blankets and were itching like all fury."

I bet Mama was overjoyed by Aunt K. bursting in like that, a corner of my mind thought, along with worrying over Pa. "He'll probably be home real soon." She obviously intended to wait, and she made me nervous. "Won't you sit down, Aunt Kate, and have a cup of tea?"

Aunt Kate cast a disparaging glance at the remains of my own afternoon snack. "Eating between meals an unhealthy habit, surprised your Ma allows it. 'Course, with her out gallivanting, I don't suppose she knows what any of you are up to."

Mama's working at the school is scarcely gallivanting, I thought, smouldering, but I held my tongue. And I was glad I did, for in a few minutes Pa and Mama did walk in, shepherding the young ones. Aunt Kate immediately started making stern big sister noises to my father, and I could see neither he nor Mama appreciated it. Marnie came home, and Peter. They sized up the emotional climate and prudently started helping me get supper on the table. It looked, to our dismay, as if Aunt Kate was going to invite herself to stay.

Aunt Kate, having counted noses, started in upon the absent Ben. "Are you sure with all your other activities, Evie, you're keeping proper tabs upon him? Vanishes all the time, doesn't he? I've watched him two or three times lately, coming home to dinner as late as seven o'clock. He's been seen, I hear, as far off as Morningside Heights."

That was the Columbia campus. I saw Mama's ears perk up.

"If he were my son, I'd worry," Aunt Kate said decidedly. "No telling what hooligans he's hanging around with now. Cutting school, more than likely. Wind up like that Latham good-for-nothing, if you don't watch out."

Mama had had enough. "*Not* your son. Can trust my

children. Learned his lesson! Good head on his shoulders!"

Pa put his hands up. "Ladies, please! I have a splitting headache, and I was looking forward to getting home to some peace and quiet." He exited in a heavy silence, and we heard the door to his study close.

Aunt Kate turned to Mama who was staring after him. "Those eyes are bothering him more and more now, aren't they? Why'd you let him go back to work so soon?"

"Why'd I *let* him?" Mama whirled fiercely, and to my shock there were tears burning in her eyes. "He's a grown man with pride. What am I supposed to do, hogtie him? You got a house of your own, Kate. Why don't you just go back to it and leave us be?"

Aunt Kate went, amid an electric stillness. I took the roast out of the oven and rang the dinner bell.

It was unfortunate that Ben chose that moment to return. Mama swung on him. "Out cutting school, I suppose! Getting in trouble like your good-for-nothing friends. Leave me in the dark, have to find out about it from your aunt!"

"I'm sorry I'm late; I asked Tish to explain. Mama, please don't start—"

"Start, nothing; I intend to finish. Dragging your sister in to cover up for you, got no shame?" Mama flung her head back. "What you been doing hanging around down at Morningside Heights?"

"Getting help from Philip Grimes in finding my good-for-nothing friend," Ben said evenly. "Who has what's probably a permanently banged-up leg. Which he got, whether you're willing to credit it or not, trying to rescue people from a burning train. I go down there a lot, Mama. Philip Grimes has been a darn good friend.

And a lot better person than these lily-white hypocrites around here who are so busy heaping judgement on Doug and poor old Hodge that they never think of reaching out to salvage them. Now are we going to have dinner or let the food get cold?''

The rock of righteousness was definitely crumbling under Mama's feet. ''Don't want to make a nuisance of yourself with Mr. Grimes,'' she grumbled. ''Grown man, doesn't want to be pestered by a high school boy.''

''That's not true. We're friends. Just the way Tish is with Mrs. Owens. She spends enough time hanging around with her.''

I could have killed him for that, and I could have killed myself for what I, in too-quick defensiveness, rushed in to say.

''No, I don't. She helps me with my work. She's not a friend, really. It's more like she haunts me.''

I stopped abruptly. Mama was looking at me oddly.

''Don't you think,'' Marnie said loudly, ''we ought to eat?''

Peter, who was first to the dining room, reported that Cicero was helping himself to biscuits; and that effectively put an end to the kitchen confrontation.

That night I lay awake late in the dark, though, and thought of many things. I may have dozed, I do not know, but all at once it was much later and I was sitting bolt upright in bed, wide awake and icy cold. Voices were coming from my parents' room. They were low voices, but they were suffused with an energy that traveled through the walls.

''In the name of God,'' Mama was saying, ''can't you see what you're doing? So danged stubborn proud. If you won't think of yourself, or me, think of the children!" A low rumble from Pa, as if he was very tired; then Mama's voice again, impatiently. "Yes, I know you love the work, can understand that. But you're killing your eyesight. Can see what it's done already. Got to go easy. . . ."

My bedroom door creaked, and Marnie slid into bed beside me. "Did you hear?" she whispered. I nodded, a finger to my lips. "Lord God," Marnie breathed.

Pa's voice had an edge to it. ". . . trying to say I'm not needed?"

"'Course we need you. *You*. What I'm trying to get through your stubborn head!" Mama was near to either weeping or exploding. "See where your children get it from, thinking they got to be dadburn geniuses without accepting any help! *Glad* to help, keep trying to tell you that, but you won't hear it. Or is it just you don't like the idea your wife may be better at a thing or two than you are, yourself?"

Marnie's fingers dug into my arm.

". . . think you can come in trying to change everything," Pa was saying, and Mama's voice overrode him, clear and hard.

"You mean improve. You're not a bookkeeper, Edward, never have been. While you were away, I got all bills paid the tenth of every month, always took the discount. Saw to it, too, that students got their tuition in on time. Think I didn't see today when you found that overdue bill for two hundred dollars for this winter's books? Discount we could have saved on that would have fed the family for a week! Blame me getting mad when I see you messing up my system out of sheer cussedness when you can't see straight?"

"*Your* system," Pa said, deadly quiet. "Whose school is it, Evie, mine or yours?"

83

"Ours," Mama said. "I thought we were together, not opponents in a tug of war."

I shivered involuntarily. The bedsprings creaked. All at once down the hall was as silent as a grave. I clung to Marnie, shuddering. My eyes were bone-dry, but inside I was weeping. Weeping for Pa and Mama, and for me, for the mirror-image my parents had inadvertently revealed of myself and Mrs. Owens and my writing.

Whose is it, anyway? . . . I thought we were together, not opponents in a tug of war.

March

I KEPT ON WRITING, as February's snow and slush gave way to March's false promise of an early spring. A regular route developed from our mailbox, to Ken's, to Mrs. Owens's desk. Most of my efforts were stillborn. No, that metaphor was wrong; it was more as if I was an expectant mother practicing changing and bathing an inanimate doll in preparation for the living creature that was yet to come.

When Mrs. Owens and I saw each other, it was at Browning Society meetings or editorial staff conferences; we acted like civilized adults. Like ordinary teacher, ordinary student; as if the bridge between us had never been.

I hated the work I was doing, hated Mrs. Owens,

hated myself for feeling all of the above. But I kept on writing.

And Pa and Mama both kept on going to the school, and nothing more on that subject was said in front of us. I don't know whether they were trying to avoid the issue, or "protect the children."

Early in March something else came along to provide Aunt Kate with a subject for controversy. I saw it first, a fancy cream-colored envelope lying on the floor with other correspondence dropped through the mail slot in our door. I paid it little notice, being engrossed in reading one of Kenneth's voluminous epistles. Marnie, coming in shortly after, picked up the envelope and raised her eyebrows. *"Mr. and Mrs. Edward Sterling. Mr. Benjamin Sterling. Miss Letitia Sterling. Miss Marianna Sterling.* All on one envelope in fancy flourishes. How la-di-dah."

"Looks like a wedding invitation or some such."

Marnie shrugged. "Can't think of anyone we know who's getting married," she said, and shoved it back into the pile of our parents' mail.

When Pa and Mama came home, Pa looked weary, and Mama was bustling around, trying to keep an eye on him without letting on, and nobody thought about the mail. We were just about to sit down at the dinner table when the telephone rang.

Mama answered it. "Oh, hello, Kate," she said, rolling her eyes in our direction. "Yes, he's here. Lying down taking a rest before supper. Just about to eat. Can't *I* help you?"

The telephone receiver quacked a lengthy indignation, and we saw Mama stiffen and her eyes start shooting sparks. "Yes, Kate. *Yes,* Kate! Can appreciate your point of view, and I'm sure Edward—No, *not* now. Not going to let this spoil his supper. 'Scuse me, Kate, something's burning on the stove. got to go!''

She banged the phone down on this outright lie and turned around, snorting. ''That woman! You know what tarnation fool thing she's up to now?''

''Aunt Kate?''

''Grace Alice Hodge! Bet your aunt'll be burning up the wires all night about it.''

''Mama,'' Ben asked with exaggerated patience, ''would you care to elucidate.''

''Don't go showing off your Philip Grimes vocabulary to me, young man,'' Mama was starting, when Pa walked in with an expression on his face that could only be described as mixed.

''This is not by any chance what you and Kate have been discussing?''

He held out the cream-colored envelope and its contents. Mr. and Mrs. Albert Biggs Hodge were inviting us all to a reception in honor of the forthcoming christening of their infant son.

Marnie whistled.

''Stop doing that, not ladylike,'' Mama said automatically. She looked rattled. ''Fool woman. Never does use what little brains the good Lord gave her. Wish she'd spilled a hint of her grandiose plans; some of us could have talked horse sense into her afore too late.''

Ben put two and two together. ''Aunt Kate got one of those epistles, and she thinks it's her Christian duty to make everyone realize it's an insult to taste, decency, the community and the church.''

''You hit all the bases,'' Mama said, exhibiting more sports slang than I'd have credited her with knowing. ''Bad taste, sure; nobody'd expect Grace Alice to have otherwise. Point is, what are we going to do about it? Better make up our minds, else Kate'll be riding up like Paul Revere to do it for us."

"There's nothing to decide," Pa said calmly. "We always go to all the West Farms baptisms and weddings and funerals, don't we? Only neighborly. I'll be going to the church service in any event, being a vestryman; and since our families have been friends for years, I took it for granted you'd all come along. Now can we sit down to dinner before that dog takes it into his mind to steal the roast? I'm a hungry man."

"Yes, of course," Mama said with unaccustomed meekness. A faint smile played around the corners of her mouth. She was proud of Pa; I think we all were.

That night Mama wrote an acceptance of the Hodges' invitation in her best style, and there the matter rested, or so I thought. Considering everything, I ought to have known better.

"Did your family get an invitation from the Hodges?" Stella demanded the next day on the way to school. "Mama was flabbergasted. She's going to call your mother to see what she intends to do."

"We got one. We're going. Naturally," I said shortly. "Did you get your homework done for Mr. Moore? I had the dickens of a time with that third question."

This was a successful diversionary ploy. Stella, too, considered Mr. Moore unreasonable in his work requirements, and she had also discovered that if one could get a good debate going during class, Mr. Moore himself became so engrossed that he forgot to give the assignment for the day. Since we had tumbled onto this technique, history, not to mention the class session itself, had become considerably more alive.

Question three dealt with the Missouri Compromise. That day Mr. Moore asked us to argue in class, as had the congress and members of the Cabinet back in 1820, whether the Missouri Territory's admission to the Union as a "slave state" or "free state" could rightfully be determined by legislation.

"Whether something's legal and constitutional is not enough. Laws are man-made," Stella said. "To go along with something you know is wrong, for the sake of peaceful compromise, is to be a part of the wrong yourself."

"But is there any such thing as absolute right or wrong?" Celinda asked quietly.

"Of course there is!" Stella was becoming heated. "The Ten Commandments. All civilization as we know it is based upon them."

"There has to be a balance between the ideal and the possible. Between what different segments of society believe to be right and wrong." Mr. Moore was trying to center back on question three. "There is also the matter of tempering justice with mercy, and the fact that what is just to one man may be unjust to another. It would require the wisdom of a Solomon—"

"That's just it," Stella interrupted. "We can't make such judgements. That's why the codes must be absolute, and the people conform to them, and not vice versa. Otherwise, right and wrong become nothing more than what people want them to be."

It was at this point I realized we were not discussing the Missouri Compromise at all.

The bell rang, which was probably a fortunate thing. Stella was genuinely disturbed, and somewhat to my surprise, Celinda was as well. She was very quiet all the way home, but when we reached her corner she said abstractedly, "Come in for tea awhile, won't you? I need some company."

"Yes, of course." I followed her into the house and sat and watched as she fumbled with the cups and spoons and tin of tea. "All right, spit it out," I said at last. "Something's bothering you. Is it Larry's being gone?"

"What? Oh. No. I got a headache in that history class."

But it was more than that, I knew, as I waited in silence while she poured the tea and stirred her cup. She looked as if she were about to cry.

"Father's disturbed about my going to your church so much," she said suddenly. "He's afraid I'm losing all the tenets I was raised with. He doesn't want me going to Young People's any more."

I was truly startled. "Why? I thought he was much more tolerant since your mother—" I stopped abruptly. One subject no one spoke of to Celinda was her mother, whose religious fanaticism had unbalanced her mind. It was since Mrs. Dodds's departure for a rest home that Celinda at last had bloomed; the thought of her reversion to fears and withdrawal was more than I could bear.

"You don't have to be afraid to mention her," Celinda said steadily. "Yes, things have been better. Father's a much kinder person than I'd thought. But he . . . like Stella was saying, for each of us, there's a point beyond which we cannot go."

"What happened?" I asked gently.

Celinda spread her hands. "Mary Lou. What else?"

"Your father and Aunt Kate and Miss Sadie," I said grimly.

"I let something slip about Mary Lou attending Young People's and those get-togethers at the Albrights'," Celinda said unhappily. "And he was at the Browning Society Living Pictures Show. He doesn't want me associating with someone who's 'obviously continuing in unrepented sin.' "

"He's surely not afraid about *your* morals!"

"But he is about my adherence to belief in clear-cut right and wrong." Celinda closed her eyes. "He's genuinely worried about my soul."

"I wish somebody'd worry about saving Mary Lou's soul, instead of just judging it," I said forcibly. "We had a dose of Aunt Kate on that subject last night."

I didn't know what to say to Celinda on the subject of her own dilemma, other than to hope and pray it would work out. I told Pa about it after I got home, and he shook his head. "That's the view of many good people, Tish, and there's unfortunately not much we can do to change it. They've got to stand by their beliefs, the same as we do."

All this took place on Friday afternoon; and on Friday night, as was our custom, we all piled down to Albrights' for refreshments, song and dance. We'd no sooner gotten there than the telephone rang. Bron went to answer it and returned, amused. "Ben, Stella wants to know if you'll walk up to get her. Larry's departed without warning, and her mother won't let her walk down here alone." Ben reached for his coat, not looking at all displeased, and Bronwyn turned to me. "Stella sounded wrought up. Is something wrong?"

I was afraid so—but I wasn't sure where the wrongness lay.

Behind us, in the double parlors, everyone had gathered around the piano and begun to sing. There was a feeling in the air I couldn't quite pin down—a hectic gaiety that was not quite real. Mary Lou was singing very loudly. There was much scuffling and fooling, and snickers under breaths.

Ben and Stella entered, and it was obvious to me they had been fighting. Ben looked stubborn, and Stella was in one of her head-tossing, brittle moods. After a while the front door opened again, this time for Larry and Celinda. I looked at her in some surprise, and when she went to lay aside her wraps I followed her upstairs.

"I thought your father said you couldn't come."

"He doesn't know I'm here. That is, he knows I'm out with Larry, but not where I am." She was very pale, but two pink spots burned in her cheeks. "This is right for me. The kinds of things that happen here—the attitudes, the openness. It's the way a church should be. I can't go back on that, if I believe it, can I?"

We went back downstairs, and that sense of pressure, of something being out of key, struck me even more forcibly than before. Stella was playing the piano now, and suddenly she banged a chord and whirled around. "Can we stop awhile? There's something going round in my head that I've got to talk about or I'll just explode."

"History class?" Celinda asked, and a comprehensive glance flashed between them.

"Suppose you tell us what it's all about," Sidney Albright put in quietly.

"Right and wrong. There are rights and wrongs of beliefs and conduct, aren't there? That's what the Church teaches, and the school's got no business suggesting it isn't so."

"This isn't the time or place to get into that," Ben said hastily, casting a sideways look in Mary Lou's direction.

I saw another look pass between my sister and her

husband. "That sounds like a mighty good subject for Sunday night's discussion," Sidney said. "Stella, suppose you take a few minutes to fill me in on what's occurred." He marched her off, giving her a chance, I hoped, to unloose in private. The atmosphere in the room was so combustible I'd have been afraid to strike a match. Jimmie Breidenbach and Marnie started clowning, and I sidled up to Junius.

"Get your guitar and give us a concert, please! We need something to distract people's minds. Everybody knows what the real issue is, and Mary Lou's here."

Junius shook his head. "Not for this mob. Come down Monday afternoon. I've got a new piece to play for you."

But it was now that it was needed, and I could have kicked him.

Ben came over and took me peremptorily by the arm. "Sit down at the piano and play something I can dance to, quick."

I looked at him blankly. "*You* want to dance?"

"I want to talk to la Hodge privately, and it's the only way I can. I haven't had a chance yet to tell her what I heard of Doug, and besides, she's not so much of a dope that she can't guess what's going on."

I am not a musician and I loathe to play in public, but I couldn't balk, not after what I'd just been thinking about Junius. I went to the piano and did the best I could. Marnie and Jimmie, picking up the cue, at once commenced the two-step, and Larry and Celinda followed. Ben swept Mary Lou off; they danced mostly in a corner, and I could see them talking earnestly.

It was unfortunate that they were still in the corner when Stella reappeared. She took one look, and her face changed. She marched up to Larry and Celinda. "Take me home, will you please? I've had enough, and Mother will be furious if you let me walk alone."

"We'll both come," Celinda said. "I'm ready to leave, too."

If these Friday evening get-togethers were intended to promote warmth and fellowship and Christian feeling, this was not the most successful one we'd ever had.

That Sunday night discussion did not take place after all, as it turned out. Mr. Derbyshire paid us an unexpected visit to "see how the young folks were getting on," and talk about the Meaning of Lent. I wondered whether the timing of that visit was just by chance, or whether the tendrils of the neighborhood grapevine had reached his study. Neither Celinda nor Mary Lou were present, but Stella was. The evening had all the characteristics of a firecracker that, set to go off, only fizzles.

On Monday Mr. Moore prevented diversionary discussions by keeping us busy writing the composition he'd not gotten around to assigning for Friday night. I intended going down to Bron's to hear Junius's new music that afternoon, but when we reached Stella's corner, and she said to the world at large, "Come on home for tea," something told me that was what I ought to do. We all went; Anne and Celinda and myself, Marnie and Jimmie. We were ambling along, acting rather silly, when we passed the Hodge house, next to the Molloys', and Mrs. Hodge came down the walk, wheeling an elaborately overtrimmed baby carriage.

The whole idea of "baby" was the one thing we had not confronted. All of us, kids and grown-ups, had been so caught up in the scandal, the rottenness of Doug Latham, the boldness of the Hodges, that we'd never given a thought to the poor innocent result. No one, as far as I knew, had even seen him. Nobody'd thought to

94

call, and being a winter baby, of course, he'd not been brought outside to public view till the weather warmed. And now here was Mrs. Hodge, trying to look like a middle-aged madonna, bearing down on us with, "Hello there, young people. We'll see you all at the christening party, won't we, Sunday?" There was the fancy wicker carriage with its bobbing parasol and woolly blankets, from the midst of which a tiny hand was waving.

We all gabbled something like "Yes'm," and "Afternoon," and made a hasty assault on the Molloys' house without further speaking. Stella plunked the kettle on the stove, dropped her coat and hat on a kitchen chair, and turned around. "Do you feel like I do? I feel like a worm about a half-inch high."

"I guess it has been kind of rotten," Jimmie said. "Nobody thinking about the poor little guy."

Marnie smiled at him and moved closer, and the rest of us looked at one another. "What are you all doing about that party?" Stella said. "Mrs. Hodge has been bragging to Mama about it over the back fence. She's having caterers in and everything. It's going to be awful, like a parody of a party for a royal heir."

Ben and Larry entered, drawn by the singing kettle, just in time to hear this latter comment. "That's a good excuse for not going, isn't it?" Ben said. "Because it'll be too embarrassing to watch."

Stella looked at him. "That's not what I meant, and you know it. It's the basic hypocrisy; isn't going along with a lie, pretending Mary Lou's child is her parents' son and heir, about the same thing as telling a lie ourselves?" She filled the teapot, set it on the table, and ran her fingers through her hair.

Celinda didn't look up, and her voice was low. "I've

been thinking all week . . . I remember reading about somebody else being blamed for associating with thieves and prostitutes.''

There was a heavy silence. Marnie quietly got out cups and saucers and began to pour.

"I keep thinking about the baby," I said at last. "It's not his fault. And Cee's right, aren't we supposed to be loving and forgiving?"

Stella rubbed her hand across her head. "Something's wrong somewhere. We *have* to be sorry for our sins and show we're trying to change and be better before we can be forgiven."

Ben stood up. "What you mean is there's no true repentance unless it's public. Society has to get its pound of flesh so it can feel self-righteous. Once a thief, always a thief . . . I guess Doug's right, he wants to go back home and start over but he doesn't think he ever can. That's the way life is. And you want to know something? It makes me sick."

He set his cup down with a clack into its saucer and went out. Larry looked from Stella to Celinda and then followed. Celinda sat down at the table, looking very pale, her head resting on her hands.

For several minutes Stella stood staring at the door. Then she turned back, sounding deeply troubled. "I can't change what I believe. It's something a person can't just do. Even—even if they wish they could."

When I got home, much later, I asked Ben what he'd meant about Doug, and Ben said he'd just got a letter from him. "Finally. After Philip and I have been writing him once a day. He's in bad shape, and bitter. Not about the world. About himself. All he wants is to go home and make a fresh start, but he's afraid. Imagine Doug afraid!"

I wondered whether I should tell all this to Kenneth, but I simply didn't know. It was hard, that week, to write to Kenneth with my usual openness but saying nothing of what was going on, and yet some deep wariness held me from it.

On Tuesday, Bron herself brought the little kids home and was in the house waiting when Mama and Pa returned. Mama looked at her in some surprise. "Thought you're usually glued to your kitchen at this hour."

"Junius is watching the stove. I had to see you. Has Aunt Kate spoken to either of you yet?"

"Now what?" Mama wanted to know.

"Sadie was over breathing righteous wrath this afternoon. There's a special meeting of the Ladies' Aid's entire membership called for tomorrow. They want to form a special committee to 'go talk sense into Grace Alice Hodge.' " Bron looked troubled. "Oh, Mama, I shouldn't talk about them, but it's Sadie and Aunt Kate and their cronies that are behind it. They feel if the men on the vestry are too chicken-hearted to reprimand the Hodges, it's their Christian duty to tackle the job themselves before the sanctity of the church is any more polluted. Mama, you've got to go to that meeting tomorrow afternoon and cool them off."

Pa was already on the telephone, trying to reach Aunt Kate, but there was no answer. Mama looked disturbed. "Can't go to whole meeting, got work to do at school."

Pa put the phone back on the hook. "Go to the meeting."

"Edward, there's two classes that have to have dictation out of that new small-print book that ruins your eyes, and there's three new students coming in to register. I can't—"

"Dang all, woman!" Pa exploded. "I ran that school without you for nigh on a year. It's time you stopped, and I've been trying to tell you so. I'm not just speaking as your husband, but as principal of the school and a member of the slandered vestry. If I can't get a rope around Kate and Sadie before tomorrow, there'll be hell to pay. *I* can't go to that catfight they've cooked up, but I should hope I can ask my wife to go speak for me!"

The atmosphere was pretty taut around our house that night. Pa couldn't reach Kate and Sadie all that evening; land knows what mischief they were up to, as Marnie said. In the morning, when we all scattered our separate ways, I still didn't know what Mama meant to do.

That afternoon I went down to Albrights'. Bron would be at the Ladies' Aid, I knew, which meant that Junius would be at home. Quietness and music and a chance to think in peace were what I needed.

I could hear Junius playing his guitar as I went up the steps, but the door was locked. I rang and waited, and the music stopped, and after a few moments Junius came to the door. To my astonishment he just stood there and looked at me. "What do you want?"

I was so startled at his tone, the closed and defensive one of the old Junius, that I scarcely knew how to answer. "Why, you said you had a new song you wanted me to hear . . ."

"That was Monday. You always come down on Mondays while Bron's at Ladies' Aid, but this time you didn't."

"I'm sorry. I had something else I had to do."

He still just stood there, filling up the doorway, and we remained thus, almost motionless, for several seconds. Finally I said, "Look, are you going to let me in or not?"

"Sure, if you want to come." He moved aside, and I went past him, hung my coat and hat on the hall rack and entered the front parlor where a fire was burning. The house was very still. Junius remained standing in the hallway, not looking at me.

"Aren't you going to play that piece for me?"

"What for? If you really wanted to hear it, you'd have come on Monday."

"I meant to, but I simply couldn't."

Junius shrugged. "It doesn't matter. You don't have to be polite. I don't like to play on exhibition, anyway, not unless it really matters to somebody. Which it doesn't. I'm used to that. So you don't have to go on coming down here to be kind."

"Don't start that again." All at once my head was throbbing. The pain hit like a starburst in my skull and grew and grew, and the whole room wavered. I must have looked ill.

Junius's voice altered. "Hey, come sit down."

"I'm sorry. I feel like such a fool—"

"Shut up," Junius said, as my brother would have done, and steered me to the sofa. He plopped a wet cloth on my aching brow, and presently presented me with a steaming cup. "I made tea. I thought it would be better than coffee for a headache." His tea was not nearly as estimable as his coffee, but I drank it. Junius folded himself up by the fire and began very softly picking out a pattern of notes. After a while the world shrank to manageable size.

"Junius," I said, "I really truly would like to hear that piece."

He didn't answer, but his guitar gave forth a shower of sound. It was beautiful improvisation, echoing with that unerring knack of his, my inner mood. Presently he shifted into what I realized was the new song. When he was finished, we sat companionably in silence for a while, and I knew the equilibrium between us had been restored.

"What hit you, anyway?" Junius asked. "When you got here you looked like Atlas holding up the world."

Now it was my turn to shrug. "If I could pin it down I'd feel much better. Basically I guess it's Mary Lou Hodge. Everything else seems to career into that and bounce off again stripped naked."

"Like a touchstone," Junius said.

It was surprising to think of Mary Lou Hodge, with her brazen hypocritical facade, being a touchstone of reality.

"Ben's been writing to Doug Latham," I said. "He wants to go home, but he's afraid he'll get the same reaction Mary Lou has here. The whole neighborhood's split up over whether to forgive or condemn the Hodges, and that blasted christening party's put the icing on the cake. I don't even know myself what's right. And Pa and Mama are fighting about his straining his eyes and her working at the school."

I hadn't had any intention at all of betraying that; but once it was out, I felt better than I had.

"What's the matter, your father having difficulty accepting the fact that your mother likes to work?"

"How did you know?"

"I've heard your aunt and my aunt talking. They've probably talked in front of your father, too, and made things worse. They're like that," Junius said matter-of-factly, "with the best intentions in the world. I know Bronwyn enjoyed working there, so it stands to reason your mother would too. And I know it took time for my dad to get used to Bronwyn's being a businesswoman."

"Sometimes understandings take so much time that meanwhile a breach is made that can't be healed."

"You know who you ought to be talking to?" Junius asked. "My dad. He's a partner in the school, too, isn't he? And your father's best friend."

I looked at him gratefully. "That would be a good idea. I will."

I felt better then, about my problems, but I left with an uneasy feeling about Junius's problem. That night, reading over the account of the past weeks in my journal, I realized that in our meetings Junius always said the same things, I always made the same encouraging response. Was I really helping him, I wondered. Or was I confirming him in a dependency, rather than pushing him out into the world? There wasn't any new thing I could add to what I had already told him of his worth. If I was doing Junius any good, surely by now there ought to be some sign of change.

That was, in a way, similar to what Stella was saying about the Hodges, wasn't it? People had to be not just accepted as they were but encouraged by hook or by crook to be better selves. Otherwise, weren't we just confirming them in what now was wrong?

I wished I knew.

Mama had gone to the Ladies' Aid as it turned out, and she had succeeded in heading off the proposed visitation upon the Hodges. "Convinced 'em we ought to think first off of the baby's good. If we get Grace Alice's back up, she could decide not to go through with a christening at all, and none of them wanted that on their consciences." Mama looked at Pa. "Rubbing your eyes again. Bad afternoon for you, wasn't it? Told you so."

"All right," Pa said irritably. "They itch like fury,

and you probably could have accomplished those afternoon registrations with half the trouble. Is that what you want to hear me say?''

I resolved to have that talk with Sidney very, very soon.

Thursday evening Aunt Kate descended on us just as we finished dinner. Actually it was Pa she was centering on, but the rest of us got caught in the crossfire.

''Edward, it's your duty as a vestryman to have a talk with the Hodges if Mr. Derbyshire neglects his duty. Surely the church ought not countenance the mockery and show they're putting on.''

''The church offers baptism for any infant who has sponsors that are in good standing, and I assure you this one has. You needn't worry, Kate. It's the godparents who make the pledges for the child, nobody asks about the parents, so there isn't any whitewashing involved. Certainly you think the baby has a right to baptism?''

Aunt Kate backed down slightly. ''Oh, well, of course. It's this party afterwards, most unsuitable.''

Pa looked Aunt Kate squarely in the eye. ''Kate, I'm telling you as your brother and a vestryman, I've had all I can stomach of your narrow-minded, judgemental righteousness. I'm the head of this family, and I say we're going to the christening *and* to the party. The Hodges are our neighbors and they need us, as an act of Christian charity if nothing more. And you can just put that in your pipe and smoke it!''

I felt like applauding; he took my breath away.

March

THE CHRISTENING of Paul Hodge took place on Sunday afternoon. The Sterling family all attended, including Aunt Kate. Whether that was at the dictates of Pa or of her own conscience, I do not know. Anyway she was there, and so was Miss Sadie, two pillars of respectability and virtue, lending an air of solid propriety to the entire proceedings.

Grace Church had all the damp fragrance of a conservatory; Mrs. Hodge had adorned the chancel and altar with enough hothouse flowers for a society wedding or a funeral. For whatever motives, a sizable group had gathered. I spotted the Molloys, the Breidenbachs, others of our Catholic neighbors as well as the usual Grace Church crowd. Not Celinda. Her father had been adamant, and she had obeyed, feeling it more important to reserve rebellion for the activities that mattered most to her.

The organ swelled. My brother Peter, as acolyte, came up the aisle carrying the golden cross, followed by Mr. Derbyshire in all the splendor of cope and lace-trimmed surplice.

The front pews were packed with visiting relatives. Apparently among the Hodges, as among the Sterlings, the whole family rallies round in crises, and it made me feel better, somehow, knowing this. Mr. and Mrs. Hodge, and Viney and her new fiancé, were in one front pew, and in the other the godparents, three eminently respectable middle-aged relations. The bells in the steeple chimed.

"Dearly beloved, forasmuch as none can enter into the kingdom of God, except he be regenerate and born anew. . . ."

The sensory richness of the ceremony had enfolded me, and my heart responded. I was conscious of serenity, and peace, and the grace of God. Then, my eyes fell on something hitherto unobserved, and all things came together in focus.

Mary Lou Hodge was there. Not sitting in the front pew place of honor reserved for the infant's parents, not even in the prominent location of sister, which the Hodges were trying to claim she was. But hidden, most uncharacteristically inconspicuous, several pews to the rear, between two dour elderly aunts. Even her lace-collared plaid coat seemed muted by them. It was as if the Hodges, for all their putting a bold front on things, were trying to keep an embarrassment safely tucked away.

And I thought, that's Mary Lou's baby up there, and

she can't claim it, daren't show a speck of pride. How would I feel if I'd given birth in lonely secret, and knew I'd never dare give my own child a motherly cuddle for fear of betraying too much love, never dare show tenderness for fear the neighbors would remember? From where Mary Lou was sitting, she could scarcely even see. And I ached inside.

The words that Mr. Derbyshire had been reading came home to me with new force. *None can enter the kingdom of God except he be regenerate and born anew.* Mary Lou might act unregenerate, but I could not believe she had gone through all she had and come out the same person she had been before. Not even Doug had, perhaps; not even Doug . . .

Mr. Derbyshire pronounced the benediction, and the ceremony was over.

The Hodges rode in style in a hired hack back to their domicile. We walked; the still grey afternoon was cool and fresh with awakening spring. By some deep instinct, Marnie, Ben and I all stayed with our parents in a tight family group instead of spinning off to walk with the crowd. Over with the Molloys, Stella and Larry did the same.

The spell of the church service was dissipated when we reached the Hodges' house. The party was everything we had feared—overcrowded, over-elaborate, noisy. Little Paul, having endured holy water and scratchy lace ruffles just so long, was growing cranky.

"That child ought to be having a nap in peace and quiet," Mama snorted. But Mrs. Hodge was having none of that; she was bearing the infant around on his elaborate cushion as if he were some kind of trophy on display. It was, "My son this," and, "My son that," everywhere you turned.

"Should think she'd have some decency," Aunt Kate muttered, and Mama looked her squarely in the eye and retorted, "Yes, but you got to admire her grit." Which effectively settled that discussion.

As for Mary Lou, whether through instinctive or deliberate reaction to her anonymity at the service, now the party had begun, she was anything but subdued. She was wearing one of her customary over-trimmed dresses, her strawberry-blonde hair spilled into a mass of ringlets, she was a hundred and five pounds of bubbling archness and she flirted with everything in trousers.

"What's she trying to prove?" Marnie demanded. "That she's a giddy young girl or that she doesn't give a damn?"

The baby was crying; the house was getting very hot. Bronwyn, carrying Saranne, edged her way over to us. "We're leaving. It's getting time this one had her supper, and we have to get the decks clear for Young People's tonight."

"We're coming, too," Mama replied, corralling us. Pa looked weary, as I was sure she'd noticed. We walked home in comparative silence.

I was torn between hoping that the postponed discussion on moral codes would, and would not, take place that evening. As it happened, there was no real discussion of any kind. Everyone was in one of those strange, keyed-up, silly moods. Finally Bron and Sidney gave up trying to get anything of depth accomplished, and Bron went to the piano and began to play. Unfortunately this didn't help too much. Gospel songs turned too easily into ragtime.

"It's a good thing Aunt Kate's spyglass doesn't reach this far," Ben said, eyeing Mary Lou tossing up her heels to the beat of "When the Saints Go Marching In."

Stella shook her head. "I felt so sorry for her this afternoon I could have cried. Now, I'd like to kick her."

"Folks that get kicked too much are always braced against it," Ben said deliberately, and Stella dropped her eyes.

"You mean maybe she could benefit by some sunshine? Yes, I guess you're right." A short while later we saw Stella threading her way through the crowd to Mary Lou's side.

"Hi! It's nice you could come down tonight. There was so much excitement going on at your house."

Mary Lou's gaze met Stella's insolently. "There's nothing going on now except a lot of my uncles getting soused. Anyway, that was my parents' party. It's not *my* kid!"

For an instant the room held its collective breath. Stella's face flamed; she opened her mouth, then shut it. And then Ben was there, saying with just the right amount of casual high spirits, "Hey, Mary Lou, come here a minute. I've got something I've been meaning to talk to you about."

"Don't mind if I do." Mary Lou tossed her curls. She hooked her arm through my brother's and sashayed off, casting a superb look back over her shoulder at Stella, who was inarticulate.

If I'd seen that on a stage, I'd have applauded. As it was, I had knots inside of helpless, angry pity.

Stella came over and sat down beside me, breathing hard. "That girl! Somebody's got to make her see she only makes things harder on herself by acting like a hussy!"

"You don't—" I began, and Stella swung on me.

"Don't go telling me I don't understand! You think

I've never cut off my nose to spite my face? Is everybody going to sit on their hands and let her really wreck her life? Making one bad mistake can be forgiven, but to go on and on. . . . She tried to kill herself once, and I was there when her mother and mine just barely saved her. Well, she's killing herself now, just as surely. And nobody's doing anything about it except throwing stones."

"There's not much we can do," I said helplessly. "Except somehow let her know that she's accepted."

"That's not enough, is it? To accept people at their worst? Hadn't we ought to be pushing them to be their best, even if we don't want to?"

It was an echo of what I'd earlier thought about Junius. And I realized, it was what Mrs. Owens was trying to do for my writing. Maybe that was why I understood Mary Lou and Junius as well as I did—which wasn't all that well.

Where was Junius, anyway? I went in search of him and found him in Sidney's library, fooling around with his guitar behind a firm-shut door. "What are you doing in here? We could use you."

"I've had enough of this crazy house." Junius ran a chord, not even looking up.

"I know. It's awful, and I'm afraid of what could happen. Mary Lou's churning up a storm. I'll bet she was dipping into her father's alcoholic punch. Look, I'm not asking you to give a public performance, but won't you, please, please, just come and play for us to sing? It's the one thing that might defuse the situation."

"No."

Something in me snapped. "You're so all-fired wrapped up in your own needs; why can't you show a little concern for others' needs, too?"

I stormed out, slamming the door behind me. In the parlor Jimmie, who ought to have known better, was banging out ragtime. Marnie, who also ought to have had more sense, was doing a dance that bore an all too recognizable resemblance to Mary Lou's earlier in the evening. Ben and Mary Lou reappeared from their tête-à-tête in the kitchen; I saw at once that Ben realized what was going on. He tried to steer Mary Lou so she did not see, but he did not succeed. Her face had looked softer when she entered; now it hardened. Her eyes flashed. Marnie faltered, reddened, and sat down.

Mary Lou swept over and snapped off the Spanish shawl Marnie had been using as a prop. "You're only in the bush leagues, kiddo. You haven't got what it takes!" She flung the shawl around her own shoulders and deliberately, as though driven, started a fast, finger-snapping Habanera, her eyes fixed challengingly upon my brother. Ben, I'm sure, could have died of embarrassment, but he stood there and took it.

"Food! Hot chocolate and spice cake!" Bronwyn's voice came clear and enticing from the kitchen.

The crowd stampeded.

Mary Lou, deprived of her audience, deflated like a pricked balloon. She dropped the shawl and turned away, looking suddenly tired. Only Stella still sat, looking across the room at Mary Lou with such concentration that I could literally feel what she was feeling, that mixture of exasperation, compassion and indecision. All at once she was on her feet, crossing that gap between them, stopping at Mary Lou's shoulder to speak in rapid earnestness.

I didn't know what she might be saying, and I just stood there feeling uncertain, feeling stupid.

Then Mary Lou smacked Stella, hard, across the

face. Stella gasped, as Mary Lou went dashing off, jerking her coat from the hall hook, running out, shaking the dust of Young People's from her heels.

The wall of paralysis in me dissolved. I pelted after her, not even stopping for my wrap, though a misty rain was falling. I did not call out; I did not dare. I probably would not have caught up with her except that she wasn't running very fast. Her shoulders were heaving as mine would have done. She stopped, stumbled to a carriage block, and sat down on it, half bent over. And the rain wilted her curls, and the soft light muted their too-bright glow.

She had not seen nor heard me. I stopped, still hidden by darkness, feeling like an intruder watching what I ought not see. She'll hate me, I thought. But I stepped into the circle of light.

She heard me, then, and stiffened, with an almost unbearable tension I could feel, though she did not turn round. I think she knew me by my step.

"You can just go to hell and let me alone."

"Mary Lou . . . I'm sorry. I don't know what Stella said, but she was trying—"

"Trying to get me to act like a mealy-mouthed prunes-and-prisms Puritan. Like the rest of all you lousy hypocrites. Maybe you're still kids enough to play pretend, but I'm not. Not any more. I have to be who I am."

I took a deep breath. "But you haven't been, have you? Not with the peek-a-boo blouse and Spanish shawl and the flirting and the pushing in. That's an act, too. Mary Lou Hodge, the Belle of West Farms, who doesn't give a damn. You're right, none of us are kids any more, and that isn't you."

"Why should I let my guts spill out for all those

self-righteous Pharisees to trample on? Your aunt, old Sadie, those sanctimonious Molloys. Do you think I don't know what they've been saying? *They're* hypocrites, they blame us for one lie, but they lie to themselves a dozen times a day, telling themselves the judging they do is Christian. What a ninny I was to think I could come home. Doug had the right idea, get far away and don't give a damn about anyone or anything.''

I swallowed. ''But you do care. And that means something. Oh, Mary Lou, we've made mistakes, but we are trying. Even Stella was. She couldn't bear—''

''What she couldn't bear,'' Mary Lou said distinctly, ''is that your brother's contaminating himself by being decent to me. Now will you please get the hell away from here and leave me be?''

I went because I didn't have the strength or wisdom to know what else to do. But I didn't go back to Bronwyn's, not even for my coat. I walked on home, alone in the quiet night; and the damp and the March cold penetrated to my bones.

I walked along, and an uncanny feeling haunted me that I had done it all before. The indecision, the running after someone who had fled, the caring and the trying too late, and failing. Tish Sterling on a crusade she did not know how to win. There had been a girl in school last year named Hodel Resnikov. Brilliant, sensitive, arrogant, ''different.'' She, too, had been found wanting by those who had no business judging. I had gone after her, too; had gone on a crusade. And had then, I thought bitterly, no better success than now.

I felt like talking to my father, but when I reached home Pa was lying down in his study with a wet towel on his eyes, and Mama was sitting at the kitchen table grimly making out tuition bills. Obviously, there had been another clash. But all I could do, at the moment, was go upstairs and pour out my feelings in my journal.

The atmosphere around school was very strange next day. I didn't realize, till I saw Mary Lou, that I'd been half-afraid she would follow Doug's example and just run off. But she was there, very stiff and defiant and speaking to nobody. Stella, too, had chips on both her shoulders. No one was comfortable; everyone was very civil and polite. Ben was not even around the cafeteria for lunch, and when the three o'clock bell rang Stella cornered me.

"Where did Ben go, do you know?" I looked at her blankly, and she went on in that brittle voice. "He cut the whole afternoon session, and Mr. Moore's not pleased." Stella worked, during her study period, in the principal's office, and she always found out about these things. My heart sank. "Tish, what kind of mood was he in when he got home last night? Was he awfully mad?"

"I don't know. I was already in bed when he came in. And this morning he had those devil-may-care walls up. You know."

"He probably went over to Mary Lou's," Stella said drearily. "Last night he knew I was upset, and when he found out why, he bawled me out. Hard. For trying to play God." She locked her hands together tightly. "I don't understand. He used to think she was just awful. But ever since . . ." She stopped, blinking. Stella, who never lets anybody see her cry.

I waited, and after a while she went on in a more steady voice. "Something's out of kilter, something's missing. You don't suppose he's starting to *like* her, do you? Or is it just that he doesn't much like me any more? And now today—*she's* here in school. So where do you suppose he went?"

"Probably somewhere to talk to Mr. Grimes."

"I hope he can talk some sense into him," Stella said grimly. "Cutting school—he hasn't done that in months; if he starts again . . . Tish, I'm scared. He and Mary Lou—something keeps telling me they bring out the worst in each other. Neither one of them can afford it. I'm only trying to help, and he won't even understand."

She left, not asking me to come with her for tea. It was Monday afternoon; Bron would be out, and Junius would be expecting me. All I really wanted to do was go to my own home, perhaps up in the old treehouse refuge, and be alone. I turned instead toward Albrights'. It wasn't till I'd opened the front door that I remembered the scene I'd had with Junius, and I wondered if he wanted to see me, either.

But the door had been unlocked, and I could hear the coffeepot coming to a boil. So I went in and apologized for what I'd said. I coaxed until I convinced him I did want to be there, did want to hear his latest piece. All the while I made these same reassuring noises, I felt as if I was running through a scene I had played a dozen times before. And my heart wasn't in it. My mind was standing off, wondering where Ben was, wondering what was happening with Mary Lou, and with my parents.

I took my leave earlier than usual, though I could tell that that bothered Junius. When I got home, I found a letter waiting for me from Ken; but before I could open it, my father called to me from the study. My father, who ought not to have been home from school for another hour at least.

"Pa?" I went in quickly. "Pa, what's the matter?"

"Probably nothing, but I aim to find out before your ma gets all wrought up." He was lying down as he had been yesterday, a towel across his eyes. "Tish, be a good girl and call Dr. Tuttle, see if he can see me at his office before your ma gets home? And call a hack to come and take me down."

I flew to the telephone, wondering whether the doctor should not come to the house. "Better not. I may need the lights and equipment I have here," Dr. Tuttle said. "Tish, you come with him, keep an eye on him."

"Don't worry, I intend to."

The hack came, we were into it and down to the office in what was probably a short time but seemed much longer. I sat in the waiting room, wishing someone was with me, wondering what was going on. But I could hear nothing until the end, when their voices came to me as they approached the door.

". . . kept telling you not to overdo, but you won't listen."

"You sure you and my wife aren't in cahoots?" Pa said wryly.

"Evie always did have a lot of horse sense."

"She's also as stubborn as a mule."

"Seems to me I'm dealing with two stubborn mules," Dr. Tuttle said pointedly. "I mean it, Edward, you've got to work things out."

"Tish," my father said seriously to me when we were riding home, "I don't want you to worry about this or to go upsetting your mother. You understand?"

I didn't know what to say; I could only nod.

Mama was there waiting for us, hands on hips. "Where were you gone to? Worried sick; rushed straight home, you're not even here."

Ben came in behind us, and she turned her ire on him. "What about *you?* Got a call from Mr. Moore this afternoon, all I needed, your current friends encouraging you in bad habits just like your previous ones—what kind of future in that. Got to be ready for Harvard, like all the Sterling men."

"Evie," my father interrupted testily, "right now I don't care where he was, or what he did. Just for a while, can't we have some peace and quiet?"

And I knew then that he was worried about Ben's future, too, and not just because he had cut school one day. Pa was worried about money. Had Ben told him yet about applying for a scholarship. Not that there was much chance. Ben's grades had always been erratic.

"Dinner's ready," Marnie said in a still voice. We moved inside. Marnie looked done in; she must have received the main thrust of Mama's worried wrath.

"You go on in and sit down," I said to her. "I'll dish up." I started to do so in the quiet of the empty kitchen. And then I stopped and, before I could chicken out, went to the phone. "Sidney? This is Tish. Could I talk to you tonight? I'm worried about my father."

"Yes, of course." He sounded unsurprised; perhaps Junius had already broached the subject. "Do you want to come down here?"

I made a swift decision. "No, you come here. I think we need a family conference."

Sidney and Bron and Junius walked in while we were finishing dessert, Bron carrying the sleeping Saranne wrapped in a shawl. Mama's eyes went from surprise to a questioning dark fear. She swung around to Pa, her face alarmed.

"I called them," I said palely. "Pa, I'm sorry, I can't keep that promise. I think we need a family conference." I paused, floundered, turned beseechingly to Ben who rescued me.

"Tish is right; the air around this place needs clearing. What happened, Tish? Pa's eyes go bad on him again today?" I nodded. "Everybody we know," Ben said half angrily, "is trying to give everyone else unwanted help, not taking it their own selves when they ought to and doing a blasted amount of harm in the name of good intentions."

"Amen," Marnie murmured.

Mama muttered something about not butting into other people's business.

"What *is* whose business, Mama?" Ben asked patiently. "Seems to me the lines of demarcation have gotten all fouled up. And it seems to me the Sterling pride and Stryker stubbornness are on a collision course."

Pa and Mama both tried to talk at once.

"Shut up!" a voice said loudly, and it was my voice. Everyone was shocked to silence, and in that silence I burned all my bridges. I spilled out everything that I had seen and heard, all the private weaknesses and fears. By the time I was finished, everyone was shaken, Pa and Mama most of all. They had had no idea how much we'd known and worried.

"Got no business," Mama started to say, then something seemed to go wrong with her voice.

"Family problems are a family's business," Sidney said quietly. "As for school business, I'm a partner in that, too. Or have you been forgetting?" Pa and Mama both looked embarrassed. "I don't know why you didn't let me in on this a whole piece back. Actually, from where I sit, the solution looks as clear as the nose before your face. Each of you ought to leave the other to

116

do what that one does well, alone and without interruption, instead of two stubborn people trying to *do* everything and *run* everything. Division of labor's the fashionable thing in business enterprises these days, you know. Why can't I run the finances, Evie run the office, Edward run the school—with outside help on the fine print,'' he said hastily as Mama tried to speak. ''It seems to me then all of you'd be happy. For pity sake, Ed, at your stage in life what do you have to prove by having your wife tucked up on a home shelf with her tatting? Your children are growing up, your house is running fine. You want Evie to turn into a Kate or Sadie minding everybody else's business because she's got more energy than constructive uses for it?''

I decided it was time the younger generation got out of there. ''Junius, will you help make coffee?'' I asked, and headed for the kitchen. Ben and Marnie followed, and Peter wisely bore Melissa off to the attic to play till she got tired.

I don't know how much was changed by the family conference. At least, as Ben said, the air got cleared. And when, much later, Mama went up to bed, Pa did not stay downstairs on the study sofa.

It wasn't till I was up in my own room and undressed that I remembered Kenneth's letter. I crept downstairs through the darkened house and found it where I'd dropped it on the hall table. It was thin, it did not contain any edited compositions. As my eyes scanned the sheets covered in what Ben called hen's scratches, that sense of communion between myself and Kenneth grew, and with it the experiencing, in my own self, of Kenneth's anguish.

''Ever since we heard about that train wreck, my mother's been worrying herself sick over Doug. Now she wants to hire detectives to go out and find him. I don't know what will happen to her if she doesn't hear soon.''

What should I do? Ben knew where Doug was, but Ben thought that it was wrong to tell until Doug wished it.

''She wants him to come back. The idea makes me sick. All that will happen is he'll *use* us again, lie to us again, let us down again. I can't believe it's possible for him to change. I trusted, once, that there had to be some good buried deep within him. I can't believe that any more, not now or ever.''

As soon as I had finished reading, I went straight to my desk for pen and paper. And then the pen dropped from my hand. What could I say? All my impulse was to go to him, put my arms around him and hold him tight. There was no way to change someone's belief, tell him to stop hurting, give him faith.

I felt again, as I had with my parents, as I had with Mary Lou, that there had to be a way to communicate bone-deep truth to others. What were talents for? I had—at least at times—a gift of magic, but to sit down and write Ken a sermon on forgiveness, no matter how beautiful the phrases I couched it in, would not make him experience what it was to be a prodigal who needed to return.

I sighed, gazing at the blank sheet of paper, feeling as I had on Sunday night that I was treading an old and futile path. I could ache with Mary Lou; I could therefore—just a very little—ache for Doug. But how could that teach anyone else compassion, any more than my aching over Hodel Resnikov had done? Any more than I'd made anyone understand about Hodel Resnikov, and what I'd learned. . . .

began taking shape just beyond the edges of my conscious thought.

Hodel had been an alien, "different," an outsider. She had been ostracized not for what she was, but what she seemed—and it had occurred to no one to wonder how she felt. I had reached out to her . . . but to my shame, I still didn't know whether it was through care for *her,* or my own irritation with those who snubbed her. I had, in fact, almost wallowed in my "Christian virtue." And then . . . my face still burned at the memory . . . Hodel had invited me home for dinner, and her mother had refused to let me in, because she didn't want a gentile sitting at her table. For the first time in my life, I had experienced what it was to be rejected with no recognition of worth as a human being.

Nobody but me had learned anything from that experience, because I'd never told.

Because of Hodel, I could feel with Mary Lou. Because of that, feel just a mustard seed's worth of faith in Doug's redemption. I could not make Mary Lou's story public; I had no right. But I could speak out through the framework of my own experience with Hodel Resnikov.

I picked up my pen, and I began to write. The words flew from me, spilling across the page, and even as they did, I knew that they were good. It was not conceit; I was not shaping them, they came through me from some source beyond. I knew, with a pounding in my ears, that the miracle Mrs. Owens had spoken of was happening. I *had* learned structure from those endless, dreary lessons. Now form and magic were pouring out both together. When I was finished I felt as if a great burden had been lifted from my shoulders.

I didn't even read over what I'd written. I put out the

lamp and fell asleep. When I awoke, so very early that the sky was gunmetal grey, I read the story and knew it was absolutely right. I copied it carefully, not from conscious decision but as if compelled by something deep within me. And I hurried through breakfast, put on hat and coat, and started off ahead of everyone else to school.

The air was fresh, and up in the arching trees the birds were twittering. It did not seem possible, but it would be Easter in another week. The school was still clammy, though, and at this hour heat was not yet rising notice-ably in the pipes. I put my wraps away and, carrying my story, tiptoed down the corridors.

There was a light on in Mrs. Owens's room. She was standing by the window, gazing out, and the expression on her face made me grow still, made me feel I was intruding into a stranger's private world. She looked older, she looked tired, she looked burdened in a way I had not known that she could ever be.

Then she turned and saw me, and the very silence between us vibrated with words unspoken. I went in, holding out my manuscript.

"Would you read this, please? I need to know if it's good enough to go in *Literary Magazine*."

April

SOMETHING HAPPENED to me the night that story came; I broke into a new awareness. I can honestly say I did not write that story, did not throw in magic with the right hand and technique with the left. I felt, in the words of Celinda's theology, that I'd been born again. I wish I could say all was milk and honey from then on where writing was concerned, but that was not the truth. The very next thing I attempted was as dull and lifeless as anything I'd ever done. I had thought, irrationally, that once the miracle had happened it always would; all I needed was to be willing. I was; it didn't. I was more bereft than ever, for now I knew exactly what was missing.

The grey morning that I brought the story to her, Mrs.

Owens read it while I waited. When she looked up, there was an odd expression in her eyes. "Yes," she said. "Yes, of course," as if to say, this is exactly right and we both know it. She said, "Certainly put it in *Literary Magazine*. But first be very sure you understand what you are doing."

"I can't help it," I said. "I have to." Mrs. Owens gave me that strange look again and nodded as if she understood. For that, too, had happened, we were back in communication.

So, feeling rather naked in the wind, I included the Hodel story in the bundle of manuscripts going to the printers. And then I put it from my mind. Other matters crowded for attention. At the end of this week was Good Friday, which marked the beginning of our spring vacation. Miss Sadie, predictably, chose to squeeze two tests in first. I received another disturbing letter from Pennsylvania, enclosing several of my opuses with approving comments. Ken didn't mention Doug. Only in his closing lines, after he'd been encouraging me not to despair about dry patches in my writing, did he betray more than he had intended.

"Don't get discouraged, even if the going's hard. You not only have to do something, you know what that something is. All you need is to nurture the mustard seed. You've entered into your inheritance, however hard. You can't know what a blessing that is compared to floundering in the dark."

Kenneth floundering? The notion shocked me. But of course; the pastoral world that was so idyllic a summertime retreat could grow barren in winter for someone starved for plays, art galleries and talk of books. Of course; with parents whose whole focus was on "Douglas, my son." No wonder he felt a sense of purposelessness there. He should be back here, I thought, but I could not write it. I wrote instead, "You have a talent for editing, that's sure. Maybe that's your gift. Thanks to you, *I'm* able to be better."

In the same Tuesday mail that brought Ken's letter, we had one from Aunt Annie, demanding that we spend the Easter holidays with them in Stamford. "Enough of our always traipsing to New York," she wrote. "You have no crises, weddings or christenings in the immediate offing, I sincerely trust! We shall expect you on the Friday morning train."

Mama thought that was a marvelous idea; it meant we didn't have to entertain Aunt Kate, and by extension Miss Sadie, on Easter. Bronwyn, who's a perfect saint, filled in that breach. Then Mama suddenly recalled that Easter meant new dresses, which she always made. Notwithstanding her now established continuing labors at the school, she sat up almost all night Wednesday and Thursday sewing. She got overtired and cross as two sticks and had a splendid time, and the outfits she produced for me and Marnie were the stuff that dreams are made of.

Marnie was not a bit pleased that Jimmie would not get to see her corn-colored splendor on Easter Sunday, but with Kenneth gone anyway I was quite willing to be out of town. I told Celinda of our plans when she came over Thursday afternoon to inspect the pale blue striped silk Mama was copying for me from the *Delineator*. Celinda looked forlorn.

"You're going away? Oh . . ."

"What's the matter?" I asked quickly.

"It's nothing. I was kind of hoping I could go to church with you on Sunday, that's all. Papa's making me go with *him*, tonight."

"I thought your father didn't want you coming around our church any more."

"I can't listen to all those threats of wrath and vengeance any more. I'm all torn up between what I ought to believe, and what I do. There's a battlefield inside of me. . . . I'm in a foul mood; you mustn't listen to me. Good-bye. Have a wonderful trip."

"Celinda, wait!" But she had already run down the stairs and out the door.

The actual travel to Connecticut could not be characterized as wonderful, involving as it did eight persons in varying emotional states, one of them just discovering how to walk. But it was satisfying to tumble down at the Stamford depot and be met by Uncle Will and the twins bursting with excitement. Aunt Annie had the kettle on when we reached the house, and a wonderful aroma of sour cream cinnamon coffeecake filled the air. There was much exclaiming over Katie's walking skills and two new teeth, and over Mama's stylish new spring coat and hat. Mama, as a businesswoman, had been taking much more interest in her clothes.

The forsythia in the back yard was a lemon-colored foam, and pale green was unfurling on spirea and hydrangeas bordering the porch. I played Run, Sheep, Run and Kick the Can with the younger kids; I sat on the front porch swing with my journal; I went for walks alone through Stamford's prim, pretty streets; and all the while I wondered what was happening with Ken. I couldn't get him out of my mind.

On Saturday evening, after we had been there a week, as I was starting out on a final solitary ramble, Ben fell into step beside me. "Mind having company?"

I shook my head. We walked in silence for a while.

"I wrote to Doug," he said at last. "I got to thinking about what Ken wrote you, of how not knowing was making his mother sick. I told Doug if he really meant what he said about starting over, he ought to ask permission to go home."

"Ken doesn't want him back. He can't believe that things could really change."

"You never know. I keep thinking about Mary Lou's having the guts to try it. At least she has her family standing by."

A lot of good that had done, we both thought at once. Silence fell again. Then Ben shrugged. "Ken needn't worry. Doug probably won't go through with it, anyway. Come on, let's go to that ice cream parlor on the next block, and I'll treat you to a soda."

Bron had a welcome-back dinner waiting for us when we got back on Sunday afternoon, one that would have done justice to a return from a trip around the world. Cicero, who'd spent the week at Albrights', galumphed around the house like a crazy thing, the two babies hollered happily, and Junius said he'd missed me.

That was Sunday. On Monday we all went back to school, and the *Literary Magazine* appeared.

Browning Society members gathered in Mrs. Owens's classroom before school began to pick up copies for distribution through the day. I looked at the neat piles, with Anne Cameron's flowing cover design of daffodils and forsythia, and the butterflies began to beat inside. I felt as if I'd borne a witch-child and did not know how to acknowledge it. It was not till, walking to lunch together, Celinda murmured, enigmatically, "You've done it again, I see," that I summoned up the courage to claim my own.

"Did you read it?"

"Mm-hmm. It's on page seven," Celinda said, guessing I hadn't looked.

There was a curious weakness in my legs. "Cee, tell me honestly—what did you think?"

"It's *good,*" Celinda said. There was an odd note in her voice. I glanced at her, startled, but before she could go on we were swallowed up by our regular lunch table crowd. For a moment panic washed over me, but nobody made any mention of my story, no one was paying attention to *Literary Magazine,* they were all wrapped up in the events of the week's vacation. Probably because I'd been away, I felt detached. As conversation swirled around me, I stole a glance at the seventh page and there it was, "In Another's Moccasins," by Letitia Sterling. I thrust the magazine away from view as though it burned my eyes. I felt, as I had known I would, stripped and exposed. No one who had been around last year could fail to recognize the incidents, though I had changed all names to protect the guilty. I had written as fiction, but no one could fail to recognize me.

Unless you're willing to stand naked in the wind, Mrs. Owens had said, you can never really write.

I went down to see Junius that afternoon, having a pretty good idea of his own feelings when it came to playing. Perhaps because of that, we did not have our usual dead-end dialogue about his need to shed his shell. We didn't talk much at all, in fact. I left before Bronwyn had returned from her regular Monday-afternoon meeting at the parish house.

April had come to West Farms while we were away. The arching trees locked fingers clad in pale lacy green, and cats were stalking invisible insects on the lawns. As

I went up the front path, Ben appeared from the shrub-hidden recesses of the porch. "Where've you been? I've been waiting for you."

I stared at him. "Is something wrong?"

"That's what I aim to find out," Ben retorted, steering me around to our old treehouse refuge. He pulled a magazine from his pocket and tossed it to the floor. I knew, even before my eyes saw it, what it was.

"Don't tell me you bothered to read my story."

"I had it called to my attention," Ben said ambiguously. "What ever possessed you to take that stuff up again after all this time?"

I felt, ridiculously, a wave of guilt. "I was hoping to teach people tolerance, and what it's like to be judged unfairly."

"Well, you hit target. Mary is terribly upset. She's sure you're trying to rub salt in an open wound." My jaw dropped, and he went on inexorably, "Don't tell me you've forgotten she was the one who blackballed Hodel Resnikov. And she was the one you ratted on for plagiarizing a poem."

Ben was so angry that I grasped at an irrelevant straw. "You thought yourself that was pretty low—"

"Of course I did. But Mary isn't like that any more. I think it's more low to keep digging up a dead past somebody's honestly trying to live down. Mary was shaking so she could hardly walk straight. She's trying to get her father to let her go back to her grandparents' first thing in the morning, so she won't have to face anyone here again. And for some reason it especially affected her that this blow came from you."

"But I didn't mean . . . I wasn't looking at it from that point of view at all." I gazed at my brother through blurring tears. "It was Mary Lou I was especially hoping this would help. Mary Lou and Mama and Celinda, even Doug—all the people other people are judging. It was Mary Lou I was really writing about, not Hodel Resnikov.''

''Well, we certainly can't tell her that. It would make it worse.''

Yes, of course; I knew all about Mary Lou's threadbare pride. ''I'll think of something.'' I stood up, but Ben blocked my way.

''No, *I* will. You and Stella have a genius for putting your feet in your mouth when you try to help Mary.'' He vanished down the ladder.

It was not until much later that it occurred to me to wonder when and how Ben had become Mary Lou Hodge's confidant to this extent. After Ben had gone, I just stood dazedly, and then I crept down the ladder, very carefully, for I too was shaking so I could scarcely stand. All the anxiety, all the burden and guilt I had inexplicably felt while writing ''In Another's Moccasins'' came back a thousandfold, but without the joy. How, how could I have been so stupid as to not realize that Mary Lou's part in the Hodel episode might make her see another meaning in that story, and that if she saw its true purpose, the portrayal of herself as victim, it might hurt her pride? Never in my wildest dreams could I have imagined that anyone could read it and think I was standing off detachedly playing holier-than-thou. The fact that someone couldn't see that *I* was the one exposed in it was the greatest irony of all.

I needed sanctuary; I needed Kenneth; I needed somebody to pat my head like a child's and tell me everything would be all right. Instinctively my feet turned toward where I had always found such absolution, to Grace Church. The door was open, as it always was, and I slipped inside and knelt down in the back pew. I buried my head in my arms and the words of the old prayers I'd grown up with came to me with a familiarity that was almost automatic. I repeated them as I'd done so many times before, and the scent of candle smoke and the faint stale sweetness of the altar flowers assailed me. There was the gleam of the altar cross, the dim jewel-colored light filtering through stained glass windows. But something was missing; something that always happened for me here no longer happened. The same thoughts chased themselves around my brain, the same emotions ached. The same burden of involuntary guilt was on my shoulders.

I sat back in my pew, disconsolate and disturbed, and all at once the truth hit me like a blow. I knew both too much and too little. In my faith, as in my writing, my eyes were being opened, and so the magic alone was not enough. For that was what it had been, here as there—I had been seeking a magic spell.

I hadn't really come here to encounter God, but to bolster my own sense of self-justification, to feel comfortable with myself. The old prayers weren't working because they weren't genuine expressions of my inner self, but a spell I tried to use. The old forms were no longer sufficient to my need. I would have to find new and deeper ones. And it hurt. It hurt like hell.

It was the beginning of an uncomfortable week. Others beside Mary Lou had interpreted "In Another's Moccasins" as she had, and the worst part was that most of them saw nothing wrong in that. I was in the uncomfortable position of having to accept compliments for doing the very thing I had sought to teach others not to do; and I had to put up with it, for trying to explain would only make things worse. Pa very definitely advised me to let sleeping dogs lie. "The best thing you can do for Mary Lou at this point is to just let things die down. One thing she does not need is to be a *cause celebre*. For what it's worth, *I* think it was a dang good story, and it took a lot of grit to publish it."

Pa's comment was the only solace I could cling to. I talked to Mrs. Owens, and she only said, "I asked you if you were prepared for what could happen. One of the writer's burdens is that his motives are rarely understood." For a moment that disturbing look I had seen once before flitted across her face. Then, as if deliberately, she banished it with a smile. "So what else have you been writing, Tish? You're not just resting on your laurels, are you?"

"Some laurels!"

"No, I mean it. You know in your heart that story was good, otherwise you would not be so troubled now. The best thing for you to do is to go on immediately to something new."

I didn't tell her I'd already tried. That was another loss of illusion I had suffered, the belief that once the fusion of form and magic had occurred, it would continue to occur.

In English class, ironically, Miss Sadie took it upon herself to teach a unit on short story writing. What was worse, she read our opuses aloud. We all cringed, I most of all.

I wrote a story about discovering that the religion of one's youth was insufficient—I even hid in that one to the extent of making the main character a boy—and Celinda was grieved and distant for two days till I managed to ferret out that she thought I had been writing about her struggles with her parents' faith. I wrote about wanting to hide rather than risk exposure through the use of talent, and it took me three afternoons of talking to persuade Junius this was not an attack on him. I might have found some comfort had I had a mustard-seed-sized conviction that what I wrote was good, but I did not. I was no longer writing froth, no longer hiding, but something was missing still in what I did.

I felt like a hypocrite on Sunday, going to church and parroting the words of the Episcopal ritual without being moved. But in my family, you simply didn't just announce that you were staying home. It would have precipitated another family crisis and more misunderstanding. I hadn't lost my faith in God, I knew that surely; just my . . . foothold on a path to reaching Him. It seemed as if God and I were very far apart.

Ben would have understood; I wished I could talk to him, but Ben was not very pleased with me these days. He was spending a great deal of time with Mr. Grimes, and a great deal too, apparently, with Mary Lou. I found this out through a perturbed discussion between my parents, and from a distraught Stella on Sunday night.

"Isn't Ben coming?" she demanded without preamble when Marnie and I arrived for Young People's without him.

"I don't know. He's been out for hours, none of us knows where, and Mama was decidedly not pleased."

"*I* know where," Stella said flatly. "He's next door to us at Miss Hodge's residence. I saw him go in, and he hadn't left when we came down here." We looked at each other, and Stella was actually pale.

"He's been concerned about her," I said lamely. "He's always felt sorry for an underdog. And they've both got a common worry over Doug."

"It's more than that," Stella said wanly. "That's not half. I kept telling myself it was ridiculous, but it's not

. . . I don't know if he likes her more, but he certainly likes me less. There's a moral in there somewhere, isn't there? Don't be too sure of anything, for everything one loves, one loses.'' She stopped, as if she'd said more than she intended, but her words haunted me.

My writing very definitely was drying up again, and it was ironic that at this particular time I found myself being turned to as the local expert. No one in class liked risking Miss Sadie's scathing comments; I was an editor on *Literary Magazine;* I found myself deluged with requests for editorial help, and if I tried begging off, that too was misunderstood. So it happened that I, who could not escape my own insecurity, began holding literary clinics at the school lunch table and around my own kitchen table in the afternoons. Ken wrote, in response to my encouraging letter, ''I am beginning to believe, just as you said, that even though I cannot create myself, I may have a gift for editing and criticism.'' My instinctive, involuntary reaction, even while I was glad for him, was to deny that the same was true for me. And yet, editing others' work was the only thing I seemed good for these days. Editing, and listening.

I came to the conclusion that, despite my uneasy feeling that I was abetting Junius in creating for himself a private world, it would do no good for me to push him forcibly out of his shell. For one thing, it didn't work; he just went quiet and stubborn and did what he blame well pleased. For another, every time I tried, he retreated like a hermit crab. Maybe it was sheer conceit that made me think so, but a deep conviction told me Junius needed me, that I could with a moment's rashness destroy the only bridge of relationship he'd chosen yet to build. So I went on listening, even when I didn't want to, when what I really wanted to do was worry about Ken.

Doug Latham did write home to his parents, asking their permission to return. And that letter, which must have taken him a lot of guts, had precipitated a crisis. "Oh, it *sounded* right," Ken wrote bitterly. "All the right phrases, just the proper awkwardness and shame. Lot of glib empty promises. Maybe he meant them when he wrote them; I don't know. But I do know I don't trust them. I don't want him here.

"Tish, you should have seen my mother's face. It was as if all of a sudden she could believe in God again. She wanted to telegraph him carfare then and there. But my father—my father can't believe those promises, any more than I. For once in my life, I can sympathize with him. I think he really hoped that crash had been the end of Doug, that then he could have forgotten he'd ever had such a son. God help me, I felt that, too. But Doug *is* alive, he wants to come back, and the vote of my parents is one yes, one no.

"Tish, oh Tish, my father says it's up to me. I think he all of a sudden remembered he had another son and saw a way to get himself off the hook without being the one responsible in my mother's eyes. He says I'm a part of the household, too, I must cast the deciding vote. And what do I say? That I don't want him, don't trust him, feel sure he'll break my mother's heart again? Or is it myself I'm really thinking of? That is what I don't know, that's what haunts me.

"If only, only, he could come here, and I could leave. If only I could go back to West Farms. Because of you, but because of more than you. Can you understand that?"

I didn't know what to say; it was a decision only he

could make. I needed the wisdom of a Portia or a Solomon, and I did not have it. Not for him, or for others.

Stella came in for tea one afternoon, ostensibly to tackle homework but in reality to continue a conversation that had started earlier in the day. As I had suspected, she was having church problems, too. She no longer found in her own church what she needed, but she did find it in ours. When I had lost it!

"Stella," I said, finally, "are you trying to tell me you'd rather be Episcopalian?"

"I don't know *what* I want," Stella wailed, bursting into sobs. "What's more important, I no longer know what's right. And that *is* hell."

And I, standing there numbly, rubbing Stella's heaving shoulders, knew that what she needed I no longer had to give.

The front door opened. Pa poked his head in, withdrew, then reappeared. "Your mother's downtown shopping, but is there anything I can do? It sounds to me like something's mighty wrong."

His quiet assurance was like a raft to cling to. "Tell him, Stel," I said.

To my astonishment and relief, she did. Briefly. Formally. But Pa has always been able to read between the lines.

"I'm glad you find all those things at Grace Church, Stella," he said comfortably. "They're all part of what, as a vestryman, I hope to help bring about. But as for your feeling of being torn between two churches . . ." He sat down, ruminatively, and the room was very still. "I can't give you a 'Kiss it and make it all better' answer," he said at last. "It may be that, like Paul and Martin Luther and Augustine, you will have to go through the anguish of rejecting the faith of your fathers and finding one that's new. But don't be too quick about it. It could be what you're rejecting is the only part you really knew, the outside shell. The real core, underneath, could have deep meaning for you if you wrestle with it till it blesses you."

"But the ritual," Stella began, voicing thoughts that were suddenly, joltingly my own. "It's all so impersonal."

"Yes, religious ritual, like all ceremonies, is supposed to depersonalize. *De persona*. You know your Latin, Stella? Stripping away, but also growing out of, our individual personalities . . . to reach a collective experience in which we all can share. But ritual's never been intended to replace private devotions, one's personal experience of God." Pa smiled. "I've never heard of any religion that says you've got to pray *only* in the words of formal prayers."

That's what I'd been doing, wasn't it? Perceiving religion, like writing, as composed of two separate camps. Form, or content. Polarities rather than paradoxes. I ought to have known better, seeing that the Bible, not to mention the poetry Ken and I both loved, was chock full of paradoxes, which had never bothered me one whit.

I went to bed that night, and I wanted to write to Ken, but I couldn't, not until I got my thoughts straight. I knelt by my bed for a long time in the barren dark, and then I lit the lamp and took out my journal and stared at the empty page.

A mustard seed, Ken had said once, referring to my writing. Just a mustard seed's worth of magic, and of faith. But both were gone. How long I sat there thus I do not know, but after a while, I picked up the pen and I began to write.

Father, I've lost the mustard seed,
And I'm so tired . . .
Tired of lying awake nights worrying and caring;
Tired of being vulnerable;
Tired of loneliness;
Tired of disillusion;
Tired of holding out the gift entrusted to me
And having it refused.
I can fight the ones who do not understand,
But not the ones who do
And shut the door.

God, is this just a little bit
Of what You've felt?

I didn't know what to do with what I'd wrought; certainly I was not about to show it to anyone. But perhaps this was what Pa had meant; perhaps this was the pattern that I needed, to look within myself for what was missing, rather than going to church to find it, as if I were going to the pantry for a can of beans.

It became the pattern after that—this hour with my journal alone at night. I wrote, privately, to find what I, myself, was becoming, and believing. Pa was right in saying that the old Prayer Book forms were outlines only—here, in secret and alone, in my own words, I found my affirmation.

My public writing dwindled down to nothing. I was too self-conscious, not because of Miss Sadie's comments, but from a fear that writing seemed to use, and therefore hurt, my friends. Mary still wasn't speaking to me, and I was constantly having to repair damage where Junius was concerned. But I edited *Literary Magazine,* I edited homework assignments for all my friends. And I wrote to Ken.

Doug Latham had come home. "I had to let him," Kenneth said. "How could I, feeling so guilty about my own emotions, dare to judge? Mother killed the fatted calf. . . .

"He looks dreadful, sick and older and walking with a limp. Very effective. Forget I said that; it was bitterness speaking. He has made an effort since he's been here, I grant him that, and if I do so grudgingly I cannot help it. He and I will never like each other. God, God, if I could only get away. . . ."

I had trouble answering that. I had trouble with my own problems that I couldn't solve. I needed someone to talk to. Shyness and familiarity held me back from Pa. I could have talked to Mrs. Owens, something told me, but just as surely, something held me back. A barrier was there, not all of which I understood. Some of it was of my making, but not all.

I had a conversation, almost identical to the one with Stella, with Celinda. This one was easier, because I had Pa's words to guide me and because she was already Protestant. But she was, in her own way just as torn as Stella was.

She shuddered, finally, and said, "If you were forced to sit through our prayer meetings regularly, you'd understand better."

"You have to go to one tonight, don't you?" I said suddenly. "Would it help at all if I went with you?"

I will never forget the naked relief that flooded her eyes. What really had prompted me to offer, I did not know—compassion, curiosity, an urge to explore other forms of worship. But I did know, deep in my bones, long before the night was over, that I would never forget that service. It was so utterly foreign to my own upbringing—impassioned preaching, pounding of the pulpit, an evocation of the wrath of God, a call to repentance and being born again. There was moaning and sobbing in response to the altar call. There was something hypnotic working here. There were all those elements of fear and trembling that had cast a dark shadow over Celinda's childhood, but there were other things as well. There was music, a spontaneous, uninhibited outpouring such as my church never had, which moved me deeply. And there was, beneath all the alien, somehow embarrassing call to being born again, a description of the experience I had had when I felt the ''miracle'' of writing the Hodel story. I sat back feeling shaken, feeling stunned.

Was this the missing piece for which I had searched unavailingly? Each of us has a need for both form and magic, but each of us has to find our own particular fusion . . . and find what for us is our particular calling and our particular individual path to God. Was that what I needed to know? Each of us had our own responsibility to discover where, and how, we best could hear the voice of God—and had to find the courage to respond, even if the people we loved did not approve. Yet we did not have to leave behind all we had known when we found our own way. We could use old forms and old talents to reach new ends.

_____

May

_____

WHEN I WENT to church with my family that
following sunny April Sunday, everything was at
once the same as always and yet so very different. The
memory of the prayer meeting's uninhibited Gospel
singing rang in my ears as we sang our solemn hymns,
but I recognized the same honesty behind them. We
went through the familiar, pre-established ritual, and it
was no longer dead, I was no longer cramped or suffo-
cated by it. I murmured for perhaps the thousandth time,
"We have followed too much the devices and desires of
our own hearts. . . . we have left undone those things
which we ought to have done; and we have done those
things which we ought not to have done," and I thought
of all my own sins of omission and commission. The

wrong deeds for the right reasons, the right deeds for the wrong, and all the spiderweb tangles of my motivations. Towards Junius, towards Kenneth, towards Mary Hodge. This was what our church service ought to have been to me all along; the communal words were symbols that united us, but behind those words were supposed to be each person's private griefs and fears and joys. Just as one had to fuse form and idea in a piece of writing.

It had taken Mrs. Owens to open up my eyes to that particular truth. It dawned on me that I had a great deal to thank Mrs. Owens for, and I hadn't even had the guts to give her a plain apology for the way I had fought her teaching.

It took all the school day Monday to get up my courage, but when three o'clock came I headed purposefully down the hall. Mrs. Owens was usually in her classroom for at least half an hour after the dismissal bell. But I kept getting sidetracked. Stella caught at me.

"Tish, can you come for tea this afternoon? There's some stuff I need to talk to you about."

"I can't, not today." It was Monday, and Junius would be waiting for me later. "I've got things I have to do. Perhaps tomorrow." I broke away before Stella, with that lawyer's gleam in her eye, could probe me further.

Then it was Celinda who needed me, who hadn't been able to sleep last night because of something that had been said at Young People's. I couldn't walk away from that. When I finally got free, almost half an hour had gone by. And then, of all people, it was Ben who seized me.

"Have you seen Mary? I've been looking for her everywhere."

"Nope. *You're* the one who usually knows where she is these days."

"I know where she isn't," Ben retorted. "At church the past two weeks, or at Bron's last night. She says she's sick and tired of trying to prove herself to the Pharisees. And she says she's not going to darken Browning Society's door, either, any more. I'm worried about what will happen to her if some of us can't make her feel she does belong."

"Don't look at me. Everything I've tried boomerangs, as you darn well know. Look, I'm busy, we'll talk about it later." I walked out on him before he thought fast enough to stop me, but it was no use. When I got to Mrs. Owens's room it was empty.

If I didn't speak my piece today, I'd chicken out again; I knew it. I skidded down to the office breathlessly, but Mr. Moore's secretary shook her head. "Mrs. Owens signed out some time ago."

"Could you tell me where she lives?"

"Now, Tish, you know we can't give out such information."

She made me feel about two inches tall, which I deserved, but not for the reason she intended. I stood there, simmering, like a firecracker with no place to go off. And then a solution presented itself.

It was time I stopped being a coward, wasn't it? And Miss Sadie had eaten at our table often enough for me to stop shaking in my boots every time I saw her. I tore off down the hall before my nerve could fail. And fortune was with me; Miss Sadie was just emerging into the empty corridor, wearing her new spring hat.

"Miss Albright, excuse me, but could you help me? I have a problem." The startled look she turned on me told me too well she thought she was the last person to whom I would appeal. I flushed and gabbled on. "Mrs. Owens has left already, and I have a whole pile of *Literary Magazine* material that she has to have." That was only half a lie; I did have the papers, but there was no rush. "Please, please, could you possibly tell me where she lives?"

"I suppose anything is all right if it's for the Browning Society," Miss Albright said tartly. "She lives in the third house on the right in Waterloo Place."

Now I had to go; Miss Sadie was apt to ask Mrs. Owens if I had arrived. I put my hat on and set out, carrying my coat, for the afternoon air was warm. Children were playing Kick the Can in the streets, and in Waterloo Place a group of small boys were organizing a stickball game. The third house was dark green, shut in by shrubbery, and the lawn had an unkempt look that made me think, irrationally, of a dark fairy tale. But there was the name Owens on the mailbox.

As I went up the path, my steps began to falter. Perhaps she would not be there; the house had a stillness to it that made it seem as if no one was home. But as I put my foot on steps that creaked, I saw that the door was half-ajar, and music floated scratchily from the gramophone.

I stood there, with my hand upon the bell, and could not turn it. I wanted to run. And then the door opened farther, with a squeak, and a voice said, "Well, well, if it isn't Goldilocks."

A man stood there, a man who had once been handsome but whose features were now blurred, as though a careless hand had smudged across a pastel portrait. His auburn hair was just a shade too long; he wore what could have been a stylish beard. His voice was slurred, though whether that was the result of the glass in his hand I could not say.

"I'm sorry . . . I was looking for Mrs. Owens. . . ."

"Mrs. Owens is not at home. Mrs. Owens is very seldom home. Mama Bear is out being the valiant lady and earning daily bread. Hyacinths, you see, are no longer enough to feed her soul. Would you care to step into the den and wait with Papa Bear? He is very, very used to waiting."

None of this is real, my mind told me numbly. This is some awful nightmare from which I will awaken. And then a voice behind me said, "Why, Tish!"

Mrs. Owens stood there, my Mrs. Owens, with her immaculate shirtwaist and soft grey skirt and dark wings of hair. Mrs. Owens, in a fluid, unobtrusive movement had stepped between me and the man. She was saying with warmth and calmness, "How nice to see you! Let us take a walk down the street together, shall we? It is far too beautiful a day to go indoors."

Her hand was tucked through my arm, steering me down into the public walk. "My husband is a composer," Mrs. Owens said quietly. "It is best if we do not interrupt him while he is at his work. You understand."

Yes, I understood—about immersion in creative labor, and about much more. The sun was shining, but my bones were cold.

"But we ought to be talking about what brought you here." Mrs. Owens smiled. "What is it, Tish? Something good, I trust."

"Yes, very good. I finally realized what you've been trying to teach me about form and magic . . . and not just in writing. I wanted to say thank you, and apologize about. . . . '' The lump in my throat kept the words from coming out, but it didn't matter. All at once I knew what to do, something that she needed now far more than words. I threw my arms around her and hugged her hard, tight, as I would have Celinda when she was webbed by shadows. And then I was running, running toward Tremont Street. I could feel her eyes following me as I ran away.

I wanted to go home, but it was Monday afternoon and Junius waited. I found myself carrying on an inner dialogue with Junius as I walked along, and it made me angry. Why should I have to justify my lateness or non-appearance to him? Because, drat it, I cared about how he felt, and I didn't want him thinking I came grudgingly or from a sense of duty . . . even if that last was sometimes true. If only, I thought despairingly, he'd get up some gumption, make some other friends besides me.

I could hear him playing, the Bach fugue he always played when he was blue, as I went up the steps. Then the music stopped, and he was standing in the doorway regarding me. ''Well, well,'' he said.

Suddenly, crazily, as though the words had triggered an involuntary response within my brain, I saw Junius, but not Junius only. Superimposed upon his face, like paired pictures in a stereopticon, were the blurred features of Mrs. Owens's husband. Both of them waiting to music—for someone to come, for something to happen, bitter when it did not. Waiting for life, rather than living it. I felt as if I were looking into the future, and it chilled my soul.

''What are doing cooped up inside!'' I exclaimed. ''It's a gorgeous day, too great to be indoors.''

"I was under the impression you were coming down."

"Why didn't you come looking for me? Or go out with someone else? We don't own each other's time. If I came running here for comfort, and you weren't around, I'd be awfully disappointed, but it wouldn't be the end of my whole world!"

"Nobody asked you to become my world! You were the one who pushed there in the first place!"

Our voices were rising; a couple of kids playing in the street looked up with interest. We stared at each other, and when I spoke again, my voice was hoarse and faltering. "I guess we'd—better go inside—if you still want to."

Junius stepped aside and held the door for me, and when I entered the parlor he went to put the kettle on for tea. The tray was all ready and waiting, I noticed, glancing through. He had got out Bron's wedding silver pot, and his own mother's eggshell cups. I looked away. He brought the tea in, and we drank in silence.

Junius cleared his throat. "You don't have to come down here if you don't want to. As a matter of fact, I'd rather not have you at all than have you come this way."

"It isn't that!" I took a deep breath. "We're so different, how can I make you understand? I've got a lot of other friends, we all matter to each other in different ways. I can't have whole blocks of time sewed up in just one direction, because suppose somebody comes along and needs me? Suppose I need something else and can't go after it, because it'll make you feel hurt and me feel guilty? And I need fresh air!"

"I didn't know I was suffocating you."

"You're not—at least not all the time. Often you *are* my air. But don't you see, we can't just go on breathing each other's air or it goes stale for both of us. I need time to myself, time for other people, for my writing. That's another difference between us. We both have gifts, but *I've* got to use mine, got to share it with others. That's why it matters so much that Mrs. Owens. . . ."

"Mrs. Owens!" Junius made a brusque gesture. "Anybody'd think you had a schoolgirl crush on Mrs. Owens."

I grew very still. "Marguerite Finchler Owens is a wonderful woman, and I'm very grateful. . . . Why are you looking at me like that?"

"What did you just call her?"

"That's her full name. I saw it written once on the flyleaf of a book she owned."

"Sounds like a made-up one. It would be a pretty impressive handle for an author."

"She doesn't write, but she understands as if she did. That's why it means so much. . . . Oh, Junius, I do so wish you felt toward your music as I do about my writing."

"I wish to God," Junius said distinctly, "that I'd never let you know about that damn music."

"Maybe I shouldn't come here," I said slowly. "It doesn't seem to be doing you any good. If it's even making you hate your music. . . . I've tried and tried to make you believe in it, to make you use it, but it hasn't helped, has it? It's made things worse."

"My music! My music!" Junius mimicked savagely. "That's the only thing you care about here, isn't it? Other people getting to hear my music! It's my playing the music that matters to you, not me at all." I stared at

146

him and he added, "I'd be a fool, wouldn't I, if I ever *did* give in to what you want? Because then you'd have accomplished what you really came for, and you'd come no more."

What a stupid fool I'd been! It wasn't my encouragement of his talent that Junius had needed or wanted, but my encouragement of him. As a person; perhaps more that as just a person. He had asked me to go out with him at Christmastime, before we'd known that Kenneth would be there.

Junius, I'm sorry, I thought silently. For more than you know. I was thinking of what would be good for you, but not really of how you felt at all. Just as I'd been partially guilty of the same thing with Mary Hodge. I'd done an even worse thing with Mrs. Owens. I'd used her; that was what it came down to. I'd accepted unthinkingly her openness to my needs, without ever thinking of her as a person with a life of her own, demands upon her, need for understanding.

"I'm sorry," I said aloud. "Maybe I'd better go. Junius, I never meant to hurt you. I don't know whether you'll want me to come again."

"I don't want friendship from pity, or from duty!"

"*Well, neither do I!*" I took a deep breath. "Look, maybe what we should both do is start over. Because you *are* my friend, you've meant a lot to me. But it's not good for either of us to live in sanctuaries. Treehouses are great, but real life's out in the streets. That's what we've got to do, get out in sunlight—"

"Together?" Junius said evenly. It was a challenge. I hesitated, torn. And then I was saved by a sound that I did not expect.

It was the front door opening. We stood, frozen into immobility, as footsteps crossed the hall.

Celinda stood there, astonished, in the archway, carrying a pile of books. "I'm sorry," she said at last. "I didn't know that anyone was here. Bron lent me some books for my term paper, and she said I could leave them in the study, even though she wasn't home." Her eyes flicked, in the loaded silence, from one of us to the other. Celinda has never been one for whom one has to draw a diagram. "I'm sorry," she repeated, put down the books, and left.

The paralysis in my legs receded. "I'm going, too. We've said too much already for one day. We need time to think." I ran out after Celinda.

She was already halfway up the street, but she heard me coming and turned to wait. She didn't say a word or ask a thing; she wouldn't. It was I who spoke, too quickly, clumsily. "I've been going down there some afternoons; we've been working on some things together. Celinda—don't tell anybody, please."

'You know I won't," Celinda said quietly. Her eyes were gentle, but whether she intended it or not, there was something in them that judged me, and I had been found wanting. Whether it was my relationship with Junius, my motives for it, or my hiding it, I did not know.

I wanted desperately that night to talk to Pa. But I felt I couldn't. It was not through embarrassment or guilt, but because it would mean revealing things about others I had no right to tell. I wrote for an hour in my journal, and that helped some; but I could not hammer out the solution to the problem with Junius, or to my own need. For the fact was that I was very fond of Junius, cared very much about him, but he wasn't Kenneth, never could be Ken. Finally I found myself writing out of a deeper need:

148

We sit and talk across a cup of tea,
I feel your eyes meet mine and hear your voice
Weave its familiar magic over me,
That tells me human hearts can yet rejoice;
That we're not given loads too great to bear;
That all our trials—and joys—are made to share;
That you have felt this same unease I've known.
You calm my restless spirit with your own
Serenity, that wraps me in its spell,
Warm as the tea we drink, close as your hand
Across the table holding mine. I tell
The hidden secrets no one understands,
And always they are understood by you.
Sometimes it almost seems as if you knew
My inmost thoughts. You seem to know me far,
Far better than I know myself. You are
The only one to whom my heart can turn
For comfort, unafraid, and unashamed
Of its own weakness. And when you have learned
My secret griefs, you take the words I've framed
With trembling lips and give them faith and hope.
You see into my heart, and you are kind.
When in the black of mind's despair I grope,
For comfort, yours the hand I always find.
Outside the misted window rain beat down
Upon the shining city streets now drowned
In silver rivers bright as are the tears
That come to wash away my groundless fears
Which, being shared with you, can cease to be.
I dry my eyes with bittersweet and rue.
You smile, and hold my hand, and pour the tea,
And tell me I have done as much for you.

How often in the night I try to find

That same serenity and peace of mind
You gave me then. I need you now. I yearn
To touch your hand, and yet—will you return?

One thing was certain—I had better not show that poem to Ken, until I was sure in my own heart what was right.

But I could show it to Mrs. Owens, and I did. I felt as if I could say anything to her. I wrote a letter telling her what I had not put into words that day, how the doors she'd forced me through had led to sunlight that illuminated not my writing only. I told her of my realization that I *had* to write, not just for myself nor for others, but because there was something in me that compelled it.

Mrs. Owens nodded. "That is the true surrender of the artist. It's not that he commits himself, but that he *is* committed. His only choice is whether he uses his gifts well or poorly and for good or ill."

"That's what I've learned this winter . . . that I may give up on my writing—for many reasons—and that the magic may go dead on me, but I'm still caught, the need for it will never let me go."

Mrs. Owens smiled, but her eyes were almost sad. "Then you have entered into your inheritance. You'll have a tough row to hoe, Tish, and I hope for your sake you find some friends who understand, for the hard truth is that the majority of the world will not."

I wondered if she was thinking of Mr. Owens, but that was the one subject we never touched on.

I don't know what I would have done, as April lengthened into May, without those talks on quiet afternoons when the other students all had gone. My missing Ken was like a raw nerve, constantly alert. Junius and I were talking only warily, trying to recommence a relationship that had gone awry and not knowing how. I felt, though perhaps it was only imagination, a constraint between me and Celinda. And my writing was dry and uneven.

I told Mrs. Owens about the backlash "In Another's Moccasins" had caused, and she understood, as Ben had not, what I was feeling. I told her the uncomfortableness of wondering if I was unconsciously using friends as grist for my writer's mill, and she understood that too.

"You must always remember, Tish, that words pouring out onto paper is only part of the creative process. There is always the time of gestation, too. And the time of dormancy. Haven't you ever looked at a garden in winter when everything seems dead? Under the blanket of snow, life still is stirring, waiting till thaw and warmth bring it to its perfect bloom. That period of cold and frost is needed."

"I guess it's my Puritan conscience. I feel so useless, to be sitting around writing nothing, or to be trying to write and not have the magic come."

"Don't confuse waiting for insight with doing nothing. It's the difference between sitting behind shut doors and sitting in an open doorway, ready and alive to whatever voice may speak, whatever vision comes. Often action without insight is worse than none at all."

It occurred to me there was a lot of truth in this for relationships as well.

I went home after this particular conversation to discover it was very late indeed and we had been inflicted with Aunt Kate and Miss Sadie as guests for dinner. Mama was not at all pleased about the hour of my appearance.

"What do you manage to find to do, hanging around

school building till all hours? When I was your age, couldn't wait to get out of there.''

"I'm sorry, Mama, I am, truly. I was talking to Mrs. Owens.''

"S'pose you're getting yourself up to your neck in Browning Society again," Mama asked. "All well and good in proper proportion. *You* go overboard. Seems mighty peculiar to me, Mrs. Owens encouraging you in it. Grown woman, family of her own, should think she'd have better uses for her time than being pestered by a bunch of young ones dancing around.''

"Mama, that's not fair! She's a nice person, and she cares about us.'' Was I lying in allowing the impression to stand that these were Browning Society sessions, rather than talks with me alone? "She's been a lot of help to me,'' I said stubbornly.

Miss Sadie sniffed. "Maggie Owens is a strange woman. She's been teaching here five years now, and nobody's managed to figure her out or find out beans about her.'' The image of the unkempt house and the slurred-voiced man rose in my mind, but I held my tongue. "Personally, I've always felt that encouraging any personal intimacy with one's students is most unwise.''

"Sometimes being able to be friends with a teacher really helps. Look at Ben and Mr. Grimes.'' That was a mistake. Ben shot me a baleful look, and Sadie and Kate were off after this new topic like terriers running down a rat.

"Another thing . . . unsuitable . . . why should he have leave of absence to go nattering off to classes at his age? Never did things like that in my day. . . . ''

"If you want to know what I think,'' Aunt Kate said decidedly, regardless of the fact that no one did, "I always wondered if there wasn't some hanky-panky between him and Maggie Owens, 'neath all that Browning Society brouhaha last year. Good smoke screen; didn't have to spend quite so much time consulting; understand she's gone on getting advice from him this year. Should think you'd think twice, Edward, before letting your young ones spend so much time with them.''

Ben and I sat appalled. Fortunately, before we found our tongues, Mama had become a mother hen defending her young. "Ashamed of you, Kate! Nice people, both of them, else we wouldn't let—should have thought we'd had enough mud-slinging around this neighborhood this year!''

Unfortunately Kate and Sadie were not alone in commenting on the amount of time I spent with Mrs. Owens. I heard, around Browning Society editorial meetings, the unmistakable murmurs of "teacher's pet." I had a clash with the senior editor over one particular magazine proposal; and when I suggested submitting the matter to Mrs. Owens for decision, Stella muttered under her breath that naturally Mrs. Owens would side with me. I shut up fast. Miss Sadie had a point: when a teacher and a student had a private, outside friendship, there were shoals involved.

Browning Society, at least, was rolling merrily along. Buoyed by the success of the Living Pictures Show, the membership decided it would be a splendid idea to hold a Maytime dance. "And naturally," Mrs. Owens murmured wryly, "no one thought there would be any difficulty in holding it the same day as the *Literary Magazine* goes to the printers. I can't blame their wanting to celebrate the work's being done, but nobody ever seems to realize that celebration, too, is work.''

We were talking in private, after the others all had

gone, and it was then I had my bright idea. "You know who *doesn't* have any responsibility with *Literary Magazine,* and who *could* do it? Mary Hodge. No, I mean it. She worked like a dog, when she was allowed to, on the Living Pictures Show; and she needs something to make people recognize that she can be responsible. If you talked to her, seriously . . . I have an idea you could do better on the subject of peek-a-boo blouses than Stella or me."

That was Tuesday. On Wednesday it became known that Mary Hodge had been appointed chairman of the dance, and on Thursday Bron telephoned for me to come to tea and tell her what the dickens was going on. "Sadie was over here last night, fuming like a firecracker ready to go off and making her same old speech about morality and corruption. You'd better let me in on what's happening in Browning Society inner circles, so I can deal with her when she lands in here again."

I groaned. "It was all my idea, but don't you say so! I don't want a run-in with Mary or Ben again!" I outlined what had been behind my thinking, and Bron said, "Hmm," comprehensively.

"You don't think there's going to be more trouble?"

"Where you have a Hodge and a Sadie Albright," Bron said starkly, "heavy storm warnings are inevitable. You're right; if it works out well, it could be the best thing possible. But I think we'd all better say some prayers."

When I looked for Mrs. Owens after school on Friday, she was nowhere to be found. By that time I was sure Stella and Celinda both had gone; and I walked home alone, slowly, through a grey and sodden rain. It bent the branches of the lilacs so that their lavender blossoms drooped forlornly. Last year at this time, Ken and I had been playing Romeo and Juliet, there had been no scandal, and my grandfather had not died.

When I reached home, there was a letter from Kenneth waiting. He was the lowest he had ever been; he, too, had been thinking of last spring. Things were not going well between him and Doug. "Not because we do not try; we do, but too much hangs between us. Honest to God, I think it would be better for all of us if I was not here. It has just struck me why I get such a downward pull of death and suffocation here. The whole circle of people I see have all stopped growing—feel no need for growing—do not want to. Some bone-deep instinct must be telling me to run from that as from the plague. There are no wells of life for me here. I simply cannot work—or live—in a vacuum any more. All my energies are sapped by the fight against this downward pull. And when I look ahead and see looming before me the empty years. . . ."

The young headmaster who had been Ken's one confidant had left the school and been replaced by an elderly woman who reminded him all too much of Miss Sadie. He was at the end of his rope; he, too, remembered New Year's Eve. "Sometimes, I think, I could put up with all this if we were just in walking distance of each other, if we could sit down in your kitchen across a cup of tea on rainy afternoons. . . ."

I went to the kitchen and put the kettle on, and I tried to write, but I couldn't. Peter was constructing a school project in the middle of the parlor floor, and in the dining room Marnie and Jimmie were playing cards.

Ben came in; he was soaked to the skin and he looked very much upset. "I've got to talk to you."

"What's the matter?"

He cast a comprehensive look around. "Not here, it's

too public." He hustled me up to the attic and shut the door. "You're so close to your precious Mrs. Owens, will you kindly tell me what the hell is going on?"

I stared at him blankly, and he went on, "First Mary's chairman of the dance, which is a ten-days' wonder. Correction, *two* days, because she isn't any more. Mr. Moore took her into his office this afternoon and informed her that her services were no longer needed."

"Oh, Ben, no."

"Oh, yes," Ben said savagely. "I guess I shouldn't blame the poor guy so much, he's probably getting shot at from all directions. And it sounds as if he really was trying to protect Mary from the same. But why in the name of Ned make her chairman in the first place, and then back down?"

My heart sank. "It seemed like such a good idea."

"Not one of yours again? I might have known. Look, tell me straight out what the story is, far as you know. I made Mary promise to sit tight till I found out. We may have to drag Mrs. Owens in to interpret to her. The kid can't take much more. And," Ben said hotly, "she dang well shouldn't have to. This community's had its pound of flesh."

Footsteps pounded up the stairs, and there was banging on the door Ben prudently had locked. "Ben! Tish! Are you in there?"

"That's Stella!" I threw open the door, and she tumbled in. She, too, was soaked.

"I've been trying to get you on the phone, but Marnie had the line tied up. . . . Mary Lou left her house with a suitcase, and I think she's trying to run away. I tried to talk to her, but she wouldn't listen. Ben, I couldn't think of anyone but you who could make her hear. . . ."

Stella was trembling, and not from cold alone. I said, "Sit down," and pushed a chair beneath her. Ben pelted down the stairs, calling back over his shoulder, "You two stay here."

It was very still in the attic after he had gone. "I'll make some tea," I said.

Stella shook her head. "No, I don't want it." She didn't want to borrow dry clothes, either, so I wrapped an old blanket around her, and we waited, staring out the window at the steadily falling rain.

After a while Stella stopped shaking. She pushed the blankets back. "I'm going. I'd just as leave not be here when he—oh, rats, you know."

Yes, I did. It had cost a lot, what Stella had done, and I had never admired her more.

"I'll let you know what happens," I said, carefully casual; and she said, "You do that," and went. Time ticked by. Mama telephoned to say she and Pa were working late. Jimmie Breidenbach invited himself to stay for supper. At last the door opened and Ben entered, steering Mary Hodge before him. He had a firm grip on her elbow with one hand, and with the other he carried her small, shabby bag.

"All right. Up to the attic," he said firmly. "You, too," he threw in my direction. "Marnie, bring up some coffee, or soup if that's what I smell cooking, and then clear out. Now march!"

I expected Mary to blaze at this peremptory treatment, but she seem to lack even the energy to fight. I thought, she's where Ken's at, not even the strength to keep on keeping on. Ben pushed her ahead of us into the attic, shut and locked the door, and leaned against it. "Now," he said, "we're staying here until we get this mess cleared up."

"What's the use?" Mary said drearily. "What the hell's the use?" She looked at him; she wouldn't so much as turn her eyes in my direction. "You've tried. I've tried. I thought, come back and live it down . . . oh, sure, there was a certain amount of rub their noses in the dust; but I got past that, that kind of thing is only kid stuff after—"

"I did realize that," I said, not moving.

"Then why did you write that rotten, stinking story?"

Ben looked at me. "Tell her, Tish," he ordered.

"You know why I can't—"

"You have to. It's worse for her, what she's thinking now."

And so I did. "I swear to God, Mary," I finished up unsteadily, "I never once thought of your part in the Hodel thing at all. I was so sick to death with all the holier-than-thou judgements practically everyone I knew was getting slapped with . . . something just told me I had to make them see, and that I had no right to do that through anybody's story but my own. I swear to you, I thought the only person who'd really be exposed by 'In Another's Moccasins' was *me*."

There was a knock on the door. Marnie quietly handed in a tray with three cups of soup on it and withdrew. Mary flung back her sodden hair. "If only I'd had more sense. Years ago. Why is it people never learn until too late . . ." She shot a veiled glance in Ben's direction. "Doug. I went after him in the first place, years ago, to prove something to *you*. Maybe if I hadn't. . . . We were like two kids daring each other onto thinner and thinner ice. And now look at him."

"He's better. In all senses, Kenneth says."

Mary went on as though she hadn't heard me. "And

that poem I borrowed. That stupid, stupid poem. What did I really care then about being in with Browning Society's brainy crowd? Only Mama kept pushing and pushing at me that you had to get into it to be a social success; that if I wasn't popular in high school, my whole life was a failure . . . I wasn't smart enough to write something on my own, it was the only way I could think of to get in.''

"I never meant to rat on that. Honest I didn't. I was just so mad at how you were treating Hodel that I didn't think."

Mary's mouth twisted. "Ain't that just the story of our lives." She stood up, setting down her cup. "Thanks, kiddoes, it was a nice try, but I can't take any more. I'm cutting out."

"Oh, no, you're not," Ben said. "What's happened to your pride? You're not going to give old Sadie the satisfaction of thinking she drove you off? And what about the people who have tried to help? My sister and Stella, misguided though they may be. And Mrs. Owens has gone out on a few limbs. Even Mr. Moore, in his own way." He let her have it right between the eyes. "You've always had the guts to wave your banners. Have you got the guts to do what Tish did in that story, let yourself be seen defenseless rather than defensive? Stop hiding behind your sister's old rag of a blouse and accept compassion? It's pretty darn hard to walk in your moccasins when there's a brass wall in between."

I couldn't believe my ears.

And she took it; she actually took it; Stella was right, she wouldn't have from anyone but Ben. She took his lecture, a lot blunter than Stel or I'd have made it, about clothing and behavior; and when I said, tentatively, "You know, one way to live down that borrowed poem

159

would be to show the school you can write something real," she only said, "You're the one can write. I can't and anyway, what've I got to write about?"

"Plenty," I said. "Plenty! You're the only one who can make people understand. I can help you—that is, if you'll let me."

Mary's eyes flickered. "What's the use? It'd never get into the magazine anyway."

"Oh, yes, it will," I said grimly. "I'll see to that."

"That's settled, then," Ben said. "Let's go down and eat. I heard Pa and Mama arrive hours ago, and I'm starved!"

And so it was that Mary Hodge joined us for stretchable stew that night; and when Aunt Kate invited herself for coffee later and seemed a mite surprised, Mama looked her squarely in the eyes and stared her down.

I told Mrs. Owens on Monday what I'd done. "I'll work with her, and I'll edit the story six ways from Sunday if it needs it, but it's just got to go in. I hope you'll back me up, but if you can't . . . I shouldn't say it, but I'll sneak it to the printers if I have to!"

"Yes," Mrs. Owens said slowly. "Yes, she does need this. Mr. Moore really felt dreadful, you know, removing her from chairmanship of the dance; but he found out several parents weren't going to allow their children to attend. If she were to do something serious, something written, especially if nobody knows about it beforehand to complain . . ." She said, as Bron had that other time, "We'd better pray. And now, Tish, I'm sorry, but I can't stay to talk. I have other problems."

It was the closest she had ever come to mentioning her situation at home. I wondered, as I had wondered every day since my visit there, just what the Owenses' story was.

I left the school, and as I walked to Albrights' I kept thinking about that earlier experience of double vision. Mr. Owens and Junius, silhouetted by a door. Shielded by a door. Doors could close, but doors could also open.

When I got to Junius's, I said, "Do you remember, back before the holidays, you asked me to go with you to a dance? We took a raincheck on it. Well, the Browning Society dance is next Friday night, and I'd like to collect that raincheck now."

Junius gave me a level look. "What is this, your good deed for the week?"

"Oh, cut that out! I'm sick and tired of everybody always thinking I'm a walking missionary. I want to go to the dance, and I think it would be fun to go with you."

"In that case," Junius said formally, "I accept. But I am surprised. I kind of thought you spent all your time these days with Mrs. Owens."

I groaned. "Don't you start that too! I've already had a dose of that from Stella and my mother. She's a good friend, and she's helped me awfully with my writing, and that's one of the most important things in the world to me right now."

Junius was pouring tea. "Oh, yes, of course. Your writing. We mustn't forget for one minute, must we, that we have to nurture every tender little plant of talent." He really was in a foul mood this afternoon, I thought. "You couldn't be working around through the back door to preaching another music sermon, could you?"

My blood pressure was rising, but I bit my tongue and counted ten. "Look, please. I'm not. I won't. Only you can't expect me to just shut off what's important to me when I'm with you. I need to share it, I need to pass it on. Like what Mrs. Owens was saying about there being a difference between waiting for gestation and doing nothing. . . .''

"Now we're waltzing round the music again."

"Stop it! I can't open my mouth if you're going to see hidden meanings in everything I say!" I blurted out, with that fatal unwittingness to which I was all too prone. "Is it any wonder I'd rather talk to Mrs. Owens."

"Mrs. Owens, Mrs. Owens!" Junius stood up so fast the teacups shook. "What do you really know about your precious Mrs. Owens? Your saintly soul-mother who's packing you so full of highfalutin' literary ideals!" He wrenched a cheap, brightly colored book from his pocket and flung it on the table. "She's probably laughing at you behind your back."

I didn't speak. I couldn't. My eyes were caught by the book cover just as a snake's eyes are supposed to hypnotize those of its prey, and the pain in my chest made it hard for me to breathe.

There was a lurid picture on the cover of a girl resembling Mary Hodge being menaced by a dangerous-looking thug. *Her Fatal Secret,* was the title, "Part of our popular continuing series of modern thrillers." And under it the bewildering, damning line, *by Margaret Finchler*.

It was coincidence, my mind said numbly. It couldn't be. I wanted to strike out at Junius, to deny, but all the while my hand crept, fascinated, to the book as it would to a live coal. I picked it up, and it fell open to the first lines. "Under the blanket of snow, life still was stirring, waiting for thaw and warmth." I could hear Mrs. Owens saying to me those same words, and I knew, I knew.

"There has to be some explanation," my voice said automatically, like a child's toy running down.

"There is. She's got two lives. She's a high school teacher, and she writes pulp thrillers." Junius's voice was subdued, as though he, like I so often, had been pushed beyond kindness by forces in himself he did not understand. "Tish, I'm sorry. I didn't want to hurt you. But you're so wrapped up in her, you swallow everything she says, it seemed like you needed to be able to look at things with both eyes open."

It wasn't that at all, I thought. You were plain jealous because I spend time with her, because Mrs. Owens and I share a world that you don't enter.

Mrs. Owens had another world she had not shared with me.

"I don't think I want any tea after all," I said unsteadily. "I think I'll just go on home." And I did, quietly, methodically, walking up the street as though nothing in the world was wrong. Early roses were beginning to bloom along the picket fences, but I did not see.

Mrs. Owens had another world. Mrs. Owens wrote the cheap pulp fiction she'd taught me to despise. She was a hypocrite, or she was laughing at me, or there was something dark and threatening here I did not understand.

There was something else I did not understand. Why, exactly, did I feel so naked, used, betrayed? Was it just shock because she hadn't lived up to the standards that she'd taught me? Disillusion? Or was it resentment that she hadn't shared her secret with me when I'd thought we were so close? Resentment at being forced at last to recognize what I'd half-realized before—that however close we were, however well she knew me, she was not, now or ever, "*my* Mrs. Owens"?

June

I FELT AWFUL; I felt numb; I felt as if I were coming down with some grave and terrible disease. I went home and sat down at the dinner table without speaking; and when Marnie asked me for the second time whether I wanted any sweet potato and apple casserole, I burst into tears.

Mama sat down quickly, saying, "Something wrong, child not been herself for weeks. I knew it."

"Has Sadie been picking on you again?" Ben demanded.

And Marnie said hastily, "I'll do the dishes in your place tonight."

"Feel like letting us in on what the trouble is?" Pa asked quietly.

I swallowed hard against the lump in my throat. "If only there was some sure-fire way to separate right from wrong!"

"Amen," Pa said. "Anybody who could put that in a bottle and market it would make a fortune." He gazed at me over the top of his heavy spectacles. "I don't suppose you could be a mite more specific?"

I couldn't answer.

"There was another letter from Ken today," Marnie contributed. I hadn't even seen it, but I didn't say that, and Ben added, "Ken's been awfully unhappy; Doug wrote me that. He wonders if he made things worse by going home."

"That it?" Mama asked directly.

Part of it anyway, and certainly a part too big for me to handle on my own. "Ken's miserable. He has been, all along, and especially now. There's nothing for him there, he's suffocating. He wants so dreadfully to come back here; he keeps asking me if I think it would be right; and I—I can't answer him, I want him so much I just don't know!"

A long, thoughtful glance passed between my parents. "It's logical enough," my father said. "He's a bright lad, appreciates city things, stands to reason he'd find himself drying up out there."

"No trouble Christmastime," Mama said. "A nice boy. With eight here already, one more don't make much difference."

I stared at her. "Mama, you don't mean—"

"Don't see why not," Mama said stoutly. She gave me a knowing look. "No hanky-panky, you understand. Don't need any more run-ins with your aunt. Won't be easy on either of you, as you prob'ly know. Otherwise, like your Pa says, seems like a sensible arrangement.

Most likely the best thing for the Lathams, too."

"I can't believe it," I said weakly. "I've wanted it so badly, it seemed like it couldn't possibly be right."

"Now you sound like Celinda's misplaced Puritanism," my father said. "Nothing can be good for you less'n it hurts. You got to remember, sometimes when something strikes you so hard, it's need not want; when it matters so much you almost feel afraid, maybe somebody's trying to tell you something."

"I'll write to Emma Jane Latham," Mama said firmly. "First thing tomorrow."

I was relieved that everybody seemed to think Kenneth's dilemma had been the cause of my unexpected tears. I didn't fool Pa, though. He didn't probe, but later, as we were rising from the table, he said quietly, "Anything else on your mind, you can come to us, you hear?"

"I know, Pa," I said gratefully. But I couldn't. Not because I didn't want to, but because—in this, as in so many other matters lately—I had stumbled into a secret that was not mine to tell.

I tried to act as if nothing in the world was wrong. I helped Mary write and rewrite her story. I worked on *Literary Magazine,* and on committees for that blasted dance. But I didn't go any more in the afternoons for private conversations with Mrs. Owens.

She knew, she must have known, something was wrong. But she didn't ask; she wouldn't. Or perhaps, as Mama had implied once, my ceasing to dog her footsteps was a relief. She looked preoccupied and very tired. Working on her thrillers, I thought nastily; and then I hated myself for my own venom.

I didn't talk to Junius too terribly much either, so it

was with considerable surprise that I heard Stella announce at lunch one day, "Guess what? Junius has agreed to play his guitar for us at the dance."

My jaw dropped. "How on earth did you accomplish that?"

"Oh," Stella said airily, very much the efficient manager, "I remembered how he played at our house New Year's Eve, so I just went and asked him." There was a look in her eyes that puzzled and intrigued me.

I'd been avoiding Junius's private company ever since that fateful afternoon, but that day I could not help myself. I went down to Bron's and, regardless of her presence, blurted out to Junius, "What made you do it?"

Junius looked at me. "Maybe it was what you said once about the ripeness of time. And maybe I wanted to find out if you would still be interested in me if you didn't have that particular hobbyhorse to ride." And maybe, just maybe, he wanted to make a gift to me in place of something precious he'd destroyed.

We stared at each other, and Bron said plaintively, "I wish the two of you had let me in on this. It's no fun finding there's been all sorts of things going on under my roof and I didn't know!"

Bron had made white mountain cake, and we sat down with her around the kitchen table to partake of it. By the time I left, the unease between myself and Junius was over.

We went to the dance, and if anybody was astonished at my being escorted by Junius Albright, they had the decency not to betray it. Celinda, with Larry, flashed me a warming smile. Everybody *was* astonished, to put it mildly, at Junius's unveiling as musician extraordinaire. And I hope, I hope, I thought fervently, that this time you recognize, you big idiot, that people are appreciating you as you!

I think he did. At any rate, he got up the nerve to ask Stella to dance—three times. And they didn't look as if they were having half-bad a time. Stella had that purposeful expression in her eyes, and she was teasing him, and Junius was actually laughing. Junius, who usually in public is the Great Stone Face. A wild possibility crossed my mind; and Ben, who was piloting me through a two-step, confirmed it.

"Be a load off both our shoulders, wouldn't it, if that combination clicked?"

Junius and Stella. Well, I thought dazedly, it's not really such a crazy idea at all. Stella would be good for Junius, and she adored crusades. Moreover, she would not get all webbed into his moods and emotions the way I did; when *she* tried to pull him out, she'd stay safely on the shore. And a dose of Junius's clear-eyed truth-in-unthreatening-wrapper would do Stella herself no harm—neither would having another beau, considering the way Ben had been acting towards her lately.

"I don't see why Stella's a load on you," I said to Ben, harking back to his earlier remark.

"She's not. She's a great girl. But she's not the only one. And I'm not the kind to get all wrapped up in just one be-all-and-end-all relationship, like you and Kenneth do."

Ben had taken Mary to the dance, and there were plenty of whispers about that combination. I can't say it thrilled me, but I had to admire Mary's grit. She'd actually asked Bron to help her pick out a new store-bought dress to wear, and Bron had come down heavily on the side of simple is best. It was a plain, cream-colored voile, with only the narrowest of Val lace trim, and it effectively toned down the vividness of her hair. She still looked bright, she probably always would, but maybe it didn't matter because it was, after all, a part of her.

"Doesn't she look nice?" Bron whispered to me complacently. "Notice the Dorothy Vernon pompadour. I did her hair. Just call me Fairy Godmother."

Bronwyn and Sidney Albright were at the dance, by reason of the fact that Mrs. Owens did not come. No one knew why. "We got a call from Mr. Moore, asking if we could substitute as chaperones," Bron said. "He knew we both work with the young people at the church. I guess she had some emergency come up."

Mrs. Owens had been in school that day; I knew that, for it was deadline day for *Literary Magazine* and I had had to take Mary's story to her and wait while she read it. I'd taken Junius along with me for moral courage, and if she found anything odd in that, she did not comment. She read the story, sat in silence for several minutes, and then said, "You worked with her quite hard on this, didn't you? Yes, put it in."

So the dance was a success, Mary's attendance at it was moderately so, and I hoped the publication of her story would be as well. Kenneth wrote me, in response to Mama's invitation, a letter that I had memorized within the hour and then hid in my bottom drawer to treasure all my days. The time of final exams, and Ben's graduation, were fast approaching. And under all the surface pleasure of these golden days, my secret knowledge about Mrs. Owens festered like an open sore.

And then, the Friday before final exams, the year's last edition of *Literary Magazine* appeared.

It took a fast ten minutes for news of Mary's literary

debut to circulate around the school. The students all were stunned. And also, I was very glad to see, impressed. A couple of seniors stopped her to compliment her in the halls.

"You had your hand in this, didn't you?" Stella said to me.

"She wrote it all herself, I swear to goodness."

"But I'll bet it took a lot of editing." Stella stopped. "I won't say that to anyone but you. I think it's going to do the trick for her, and I'm really glad."

So it looked as if Mary's "serious worth" reputation was going to be made at last.

That night, being Friday and also the last fling before exams, we all went down to Albrights' and were particularly rowdy. It was, perhaps, unfortunate that we were playing kid games like Blind Man's Bluff, with considerable pawing of the persons captured, when Miss Sadie chose to come stalking up the walk.

She stood there, a most unpleasant Nemesis, a rolled object clutched tightly in her hand. And she said sharply, "Sidney, I want to talk to you. Alone."

Sidney looked startled. "Yes, of course, Sadie. Come into the study." Behind Sadie's back he shrugged at Bron who was looking at them questioningly.

Everybody else was still rioting happily. I hoped to God I was the only one who recognized what it had been rolled like a club in Sourpuss Sadie's hands. Today's edition of *Literary Magazine*.

I got Bron quickly and dragged her to the kitchen and shut the door. "Something's going to happen, and it's going to be bad. I can feel it in my bones. And the only thing remotely controversial in that whole issue is Mary Hodge's story."

"Junius had a copy somewhere around here this afternoon.'' Bron rummaged through a pile of magazines on a kitchen chair. We found it and spread it out. ''Oh,'' Bronwyn said slowly, reading. ''Oh, yes, I see.''

And so, reading as if through Miss Sadie's eyes, could I. Mary had written, as I'd hoped, a story that would make the righteous feel ashamed. But she hadn't written her own story. She'd written, rather, from the perspective of a baby. A baby, waiting to be born, wondering if he was wanted . . . and finding that by the standards of the world he'd been born into, he was not.

''It's beautiful,'' Bronwyn said, and tears were shining in her eyes. ''It's beautiful, and it could so easily . . . oh, Sadie, Sadie! She means so well, and she just can't understand. She's apt to interpret this as Browning Society's endorsing unwed motherhood.''

Browning Society, and Mrs. Owens.

''I know one thing,'' Bronwyn said abruptly, ''if the fur's about to fly, we've got to get the author out of here. Ben!'' she called sharply. When he appeared, she said, ''There's money on the top shelf in that cracked sugar bowl. Take everybody down to Lacey's and treat them to ice cream. *Everybody*.'' Ben took one look at what was lying on the kitchen table, seized the cash, and vanished. ''You, too,'' Bronwyn said to me. ''I'd just as leave no one was here but me and Sidney. I'll call Pa and Mama if we need reinforcements.''

So we went to Lacey's and put on a good act pretending nothing in the world was wrong. Nobody inquired; no one in the crowd is inclined to look a gift horse in the mouth where free food is concerned, although Stella did cast a shrewd glance in my direction.

Ben and I told Pa and Mama, and Marnie who insisted on knowing too, the whole story as soon as we got home. "The whole trouble is, she's been looking for a weapon against Mrs. Owens," Ben said disgustedly. "She resents Tish's listening to her, and she resents my and everybody's friendliness with Mr. Grimes. She just can't get over the fact every teacher in the school is preferred to her."

"I wouldn't worry too much," Pa said. "You know Sadie and Kate have to shoot off at regular intervals, and it never amounts to a hill of beans."

But it had hurt Mary plenty in the past, and Ben and I both knew it.

I had a letter from Kenneth Saturday. "I think Doug *has* changed," he wrote. "Or at least now I can accept the possibility. It's good for both of us that I'm leaving, though. We need not to be together, not till more time's gone by. Maybe till *I've* changed. Anyway, Doug will have a better chance without me here. My uncle's offered him work on the farm, and the railroad out West has made him an open job offer any time he wants it. Doug's a hero to them! I guess right now he needs physical work, wide open spaces and no thinking, just as much as I need the opposite. Tish, I'm *so glad* I'm coming back to West Farms!"

Ken's school got out before ours; he would be arriving on the Friday train. I could not take the pleasure in this I would otherwise have done. All that weekend, as we crammed for finals, the question of what Miss Sadie was up to festered in my mind along with that other, unhealing sore. I tried to put it from me, tried to concentrate on work, but everything I ran into brought it newly home. I prayed, hard, in my head in my own words all the time the public ritual was rolling along in church service Sunday morning, and also at Sunday night

Young People's, which was sparsely attended because of last minute study.

On Monday, in and out through the rat race of exams, rumors began to crawl. Parents who had read the magazine had called to complain to Mr. Moore. "Unsuitable." "Too much freedom, too little proper faculty supervision." "Corruption of our young by too much knowledge."

"Thank the Lord, Mary cut school today to study since she didn't have any exams until tomorrow." Ben exhibited his customary code of practical ethics. "One day's grace. That isn't much. I tell you; we'll go and see Philip Grimes."

"What can he do?" I asked; and Ben retorted, "I don't know, but it doesn't hurt to try."

So at three o'clock, shunning both Junius and the studying that should have absorbed me, I tagged along after Ben on the trolley car down to Morningside Heights.

Mr. Grimes wasn't home.

"Hell and damn," Ben muttered under his breath. Then he looked at my face and forced a smile. "We're probably making mountains out of molehills anyway. Tell you what, I've got a quarter. I'll treat us both to ice cream sodas."

He steered me to a stylish emporium on a nearby corner, and we ordered. We sat, sipping, scarcely speaking, and I thought, this isn't fair, he's invested ten cents in me to cheer me up. So I started to say, "It's probably really not that bad." And then my eyes fell on a reflection in the mirror behind his head.

"What is it?" Ben started to say, and then his own eyes changed, and I turned, too, to look upon not the reflection but the real.

A couple was sitting at a table across the half-empty room. She was crying, and he was holding her hands, talking rapidly, looking earnestly into her eyes. Philip Grimes and Marguerite Finchler Owens.

They didn't see us, and we looked away. "It's nothing," Ben said, too firmly, and, "Of course not," I echoed. But we both knew, with a sickness, that we had been looking upon the scene with Miss Sadie's eyes. We both knew we would never speak of it. Ben put his quarter on the table, and we stood up and left quickly, quietly, hoping the two engrossed in their private trouble would not know.

We went home, and Marnie said, "Junius's been trying to get you on the phone. He's been calling every fifteen minutes all afternoon. He wanted you to call him, soon as you got in."

I did, bewildered, and Junius's voice came hoarsely. "You got home, thank goodness. I've got to see you right away."

"Can't it wait? We're just about ready to sit down to dinner."

"It can't," Junius said inexorably. "I'll meet you by the pond in the vacant lot."

That was my private place with Ken, but he couldn't know that. I went, calling out a hasty explanation to my mother, running off before she could tell me not to go. And as I ran, with every step, there was a thudding in my mind that said, this is it, this is the rock you've been waiting to have fall.

The vacant lot was still and quiet in the late May sunlight. Junius stood with the sun behind him, so that he was like a dark blur blotting out its light. He spoke even before I had reached him.

"Aunt Sadie's found out all about Mrs. Owens."

I had no voice except for a whispered, "How?"

"Because I was a fool," Junius said bitterly. "Because everything you threw at me was right. I did want to build a private world and have you with me in it. That's why I ran down that memory I had of seeing a book somewhere by a Margaret Finchler. That's why . . ." He swallowed. "I didn't mean to, Tish, as God's my witness. All I meant was to hang onto that thing like a nasty little worm to gloat upon. Only I was careless, or maybe deep down I wanted it to be found. Anyway, Aunt Sadie did. This afternoon. Jammed down behind a pillow in the parlor where I'd forgotten it. You know how she always goes around straightening everything as though Bron's not a good enough housekeeper."

I knew.

"She thinks this is absolute proof Mrs. Owens is unfit to be a teacher, and she keeps dragging up her dirty little suspicions about Mr. Grimes and undue influence on kids and all the rest. She wanted Pa to be her lawyer and protest to the Board of Education; and when he wouldn't, she said all right, she'd get another lawyer but nothing was going to hold her back from what she felt was right."

"Somebody's got to warn Mrs. Owens," I said slowly, and he nodded.

"I know. That's why I came to you."

Yes, of course. Because he and I were the only ones, except Miss Sadie and his father now, who knew. And I, I was the one who, through my own need, had led Mrs. Owens into an outside-school, person-to-person relationship of trust. Never mind that it had been a one way trust, that though she knew me, I had not known her. That didn't matter now. What did matter was that the relationship had existed, and that she was threatened. What mattered was that I loved her, that whatever Margaret Finchler wrote or did, Marguerite Finchler Owens was my friend.

"Call my house and tell them I'll be late to supper," I said to Junius. I started off toward Waterloo Place, wondering. Maybe, when I came right down to it, it had been my own fault our relationship had not been a two-way street. I had asked Mrs. Owens to reach out to me, for my sake, and she had responded; but when had it ever occurred to me to reach out to her—not as a teacher, but as a human being? When had I ever allowed her to not be strong?

I didn't know what I would find when I came to Waterloo Place, and that, too, did not matter. I went up the steps, and again the door was open. I had the feeling, as I had had so often lately, that I was going through patterns I had traced many times before, that I was living in many worlds at once. But this time no vaguely threatening figure met me at the door. The house was still. No lamps were lit, but the slanting light arrowed through the side windows like candle fingers. I saw a woman sitting in a chair. Her head was bowed, but she did not move; she had sunk into a stillness too deep for tears, like a figure carved in stone.

I did the only thing I could do. I went in and knelt down beside her, and put my arms around her and held her tight.

A shudder ran through her, and then she did begin to sob, as though she'd desperately needed human touch to unlock her prison. Still I held her, rocking back and forth, and my own tears scalded my aching eyes. It was much, much later when she straightened and turned her head away and searched ineffectually for a handkerchief. I found one and put it in her hand.

"I'm sorry," Mrs. Owens said. "It was not right of me to do that to you, Tish, but I needed it."

"That's all right." I hesitated, awkwardly, and then at last she turned to me directly.

"Something is wrong, or you would not have come here. What is it? Tell me."

"I'm sorry, I'm so terribly sorry to have to tell you, but I've got to. It's Miss Sadie. She's found out about—about Margaret Finchler."

"Oh, dear God," Mrs. Owens said and closed her eyes.

"I thought you'd better know. She's upset—about Mary's story, and Browning Society, and our work together . . . it seems as if everything I've tried to do has boomeranged on you."

Now it was I who could not go on. Mrs. Owens looked at me and rose. "I'm going to make us both some tea and toast. I've had nothing all day, and I suspect you've not had much either. Don't worry, Tish, you needn't try to tell the rest; I can guess it all. She'd like very much to prove me an unfit teacher."

I followed her into the kitchen and watched while she cut bread very methodically with shaking hands. She showed me by jerks of the head where the tea things were, and I got them down. A fat squat English teapot two delicate Derby cups. "Is Mr. Owens . . .?" I asked, and she shook her head.

"He won't hear. He's inside sleeping, what with the drugs, and—and alcohol," she said steadily. I had wanted her to treat me as an adult not a student, and I was getting my way. "He's very ill, he has been ill for years, that's why he can't work, that's why those dreadful stories. I didn't want you to know about them, I knew how you'd feel."

"It doesn't matter."

"Yes, it does matter." She turned on me squarely, and it was as though a dam had burst. "It matters, because you have the magic, and I don't want to see you end up as I have done. Why do you think I've worked you so, because I didn't want you to misuse your gift, fall into easy, facile tricks."

As I have done, the implication hung in the air.

"You don't know, I hope you'll never know, what it's like to sacrifice your own gifts, mistakenly, because they're so potent they threaten someone you love. You saw my husband." Her eyes flicked at me, and I nodded slowly. "You should have seen him twenty years ago. Like your Ken, and more. He was going to be a composer, was going to play his own compositions on concert stages all around the world. But he had . . . I don't know; too little security, too little trust in me. I was starting to sell stories then, real stories, but he found my work disturbed his, and so I stopped. So I know, you see, what it's like to have the magic vanish."

I couldn't speak, and after a moment she went on. "At first it was glorious, wonderful; I told myself it was selfish and unloving of me to want my own world too. But then gradually . . ." She shrugged. "You know. And so did he. And at the same time his own career, unfortunately . . . I don't know what went wrong, whether he stopped trying, whether he, unlike me, had only the urge for fame but no true gift. And then his illness . . . he couldn't work, I started teaching school. Every salary check was a drop of gall to him; and yet it wasn't enough, there were doctors, hospitals, we needed more. And so—" She shrugged again. "So Margaret Finchler. Because that was the way to the quick money we needed. But I swear to you, Tish, even

178

in penny dreadfuls, I did always try to practice what I preached."

"You don't have to tell me that," I said softly, and she shook her head.

"Yes, I do. Because it's important that you learn! It is possible to hang onto at least that much integrity. You're finding out a lot about trust and betrayal from me, aren't you? Well, for the love of God, take it and use it! And learn this one thing, if you learn nothing else! Don't ever, for whatever mistaken good intentions, give up what you're born for. People like us are like Prometheus, having the livers eaten out daily to grow back by night, that's what the creative force does to you. But if you sacrifice unwisely, both you and the person you sacrifice for are devoured by the fire that burns you. At least," she finished ironically, "if in the process you've wrought one piece of art, you've done the world some good."

There was a knock on the screen door, and my father's voice said quietly, "I've come to take Tish home."

"You go along. I'll be all right now, don't worry." Mrs. Owens kissed me and turned me toward the door. Pa put his arm around me and led me down the steps. I could not believe it was already dark.

"I know. Sidney told me," Pa said simply. "Guess you got more than you bargained for, didn't you?"

I had. I'd wanted a gift of magic, a gift of a special relationship, a gift for blessing—and I was only beginning to understand what using one's gifts for others meant.

"Kind of like opening Pandora's box," Pa said, echoing what Mrs. Owens had said to me long ago.

But in Pandora's box, when the other gifts of the gods

had vanished, there was one gift left. Hope. Blessing or curse, depending on how you looked upon it. For me, it was a grain of mustard seed.

I leaned my head against my father's shoulder, and he looked at me and smiled. "Your Ma's keeping supper hot. I told her, private, but no one else need know. Don't worry, we'll straighten things out somehow. Your Mrs. Owens is a real fine woman."

I went to school next day braced by faith and family for whatever battles might occur, praying with every fiber of my being that Mrs. Owens was likewise armed. And nothing happened. The news percolated through the school slowly. Mrs. Owens wasn't there.

She walked away from it, the traitor, a voice in my brain said sickly, and then the other half of me answered swift and sure: she hadn't, she wouldn't, something else must be wrong.

It was. The news came, predictably, from Stella's grapevine in the principal's office. "Her husband's very sick. He was taken to the hospital in the middle of the night. She's staying with him, and Mr. Moore's getting a substitute in till she returns!"

It was sickening to listen, as I did at dinner with Aunt Kate, to how the sanctimonious busybodies of the neighborhood had, out of the goodness of their hearts, decided to forgive Mrs. Owens for her sins.

"Poor woman," Aunt Kate said with belated sympathy. "Apparently she's been carrying the family burden all these years. Fool man should have accepted drastic treatment long ago, of course, and now it's too late . . . guess she can be excused some lapses in good judgement."

It was all I could endure to hold my tongue.

It was a strange, in-limbo kind of week. In school,

words and actions swirled around me in desultory circles. People stopped gossiping about Margaret Finchler and showed genuine concern for Mrs. Owens. Junius and Stella started walking together to and from their classes. Ben got word he'd been granted scholarship help from Harvard, on account of its being for generations our "family school." So our precarious finances would not threaten his attending, after all. Stella brought Mary an announcement of a writing contest she'd found in a suffrage magazine and suggested that she submit her story. Mary, instead of bristling as she once would have, said, "Thanks, perhaps I will."

That was one of the good things that had happened—the crowd, indeed most of the kids at school, was closing ranks firmly and protectively around Mary Hodge. Perhaps her story had done it, as I'd hoped; perhaps it was the injustice of Miss Sadie and Company's attacks; perhaps it was the fact that, at last, the inner Mary was more consistently showing through the outside flash. And Mary, by some miracle, was starting to accept the hands held out to her. That, too, was growth, I thought, remembering Ken's recognition of his own prejudices where his brother was concerned; remembering Junius being able to play at last in public.

I hoped I'd grown, too. I was going to need that when Kenneth came, to face the inevitable need to build new bridges, establish a new relationship rather than the ghost of what had been, cope with the pressures that would be engendered by our living together under the same roof. I helped get Ken's room ready, and I took exams, and I went shopping for a graduation present for Ben. I felt as if I was living in several worlds at once, and none of them seemed real.

"It's nice Ken will be here in time for your birthday

Sunday," Mama said. "You want a party?"

But I didn't feel like thinking of parties till I knew how Mrs. Owens was.

Friday was the last day of exams. I took one early in the morning, and in other classes I wrote the compositions teachers assign when they have to keep you busy but have no work left to do. I went to lunch dazedly, and Celinda smiled. "Ten to one you're thinking of Kenneth Latham!"

Everyone knew he would arrive that day. I nodded, but what I'd really been thinking of was Mrs. Owens.

Stella came in to lunch late, looking sober. "Guess what? I just heard two teachers talking in the hall. Mrs. Owens's husband died last night."

I didn't hear the rest. I rose and did what I'd never imagined I could do. Without thought of permission, I walked out of the school. Straight out, not even waiting properly to put on my hat. It was as if I could not help myself.

She was there, of course—at Waterloo Place—standing in the small parlor locked in the arms of Mr. Grimes, who held her as if she was a very little girl.

He looked at me, neither embarrassed nor surprised. "Hello, Tish. I thought you'd come. See if you can find some food in the kitchen, will you? See, Marguerite? Tish is here. Now do you suppose you can get some rest?"

I went to the kitchen and made toast and tea, thinking of that other afternoon when she had done so, thinking of earlier when Ben and I had seen the two of them together and had thought the worst. So what if he is a bit in love with her, my heart said defiantly. He'd be a fool not to be. And she'd be a fool not to turn to him as a friend. They're good for each other, even if she was married and there are years between them—and it's only the Kates and Sadies, who've never known love, who cannot understand. I was filled, not for the first time, with a flood of gratitude towards Ken who had taught me much.

Between us, we persuaded her to lie down and, for a time at least, let go to exhausted sleep. Mr. Grimes and I sat down in the living room, drinking coffee together and talking as if we were old, old friends.

"I don't like leaving her here," he said. "She has no family, but I live alone."

"She can come to us," I said quickly. Of course. Pa and Mama would both say it was the only thing to do. And with her staying in our house, I could hear Mama saying, just let Sadie Albright try to breathe a whiff of scandal.

Mrs. Owens woke up, and I told her what we'd planned. I didn't give her a chance to protest; I packed her bag. "You come, too," I said to Mr. Grimes. "There's always plenty in the pot at our house, and Kenneth will be there."

Mrs. Owens caught her breath. "He was coming today, of course; Tish, you ought not have been here."

"Yes, I ought," I said stoutly. "Ken will know it. He will be here from now on, but even so . . . we're together, even when we are apart."

"You've learned all kinds of magic, haven't you?" She smiled, her eyes misting, but not with sorrow. "Tish, what we talked about the other day—I think you'll make it."

Because of what Kenneth is, I thought silently. And because of you. I never have said thank you properly. Maybe someday I'll be able to, in a book.

I took them home with me, and Ken was waiting. He

came down the steps to meet me and, as Pa and Mama welcomed Mrs. Owens, he took me straight into his arms. We clung together and didn't care if the whole world saw.

"That can wait till later. Food's getting cold," Pa said, smiling. We sat down together around the table, which had expanded a couple of leaves as it always did when needed. Just as the circle round it could always expand in faith, and tolerance, and love.

Pa collected our attention with his eyes, and bowed his head for grace.

It felt good to have Mrs. Owens there, and Mr. Grimes. Junius should be here, too, I thought, and Mary Hodge. They will be, sometimes; they're part of us now, too—and for their own selves, not just because of going out with me and Ben. All of my different worlds, coming at last together . . . all of my different selves. United in me, Letitia Chambers Sterling, almost sixteen, who by the grace of God has had the sense not to give up things important when sometimes only a mustard seed was what she had to cling to.

Kenneth's hand reached for mine, and with my other one I reached out for Mrs. Owens and felt a quick, strong squeeze.

The circle was complete; the circle would go on.

Excerpts from the fifth book
of the *Keeping Days* series
A NICE GIRL LIKE YOU
by Norma Johnston
Coming from ACE TEMPO in May

On Monday, January 11, 1917, when I finally went
back to school a week late from vacation, due to
what Gram called "tarnation too much social-
izing" and Mother called the flu, I ran smack into
the excitement about Katie's sixteenth birthday
party and the latest set of ugly rumors about Paul
Hodge.

Actually, on that Monday, I had plenty of other
things to occupy my mind. One of the drawbacks
of growing up in a neighborhood like West Farms,
the Bronx, where you have uncles and aunts and
cousins on every corner, is that you have a built-in
family reputation to live up to—or live down, as
the case may be. I was Sarah Anne Albright,
Bronwyn Sterling Albright's daughter, and niece of
that famous author, Letitia Chambers Sterling;
niece also of Sourpuss Sadie Albright, who'd been
the bane of all local Latin students before she had
her stroke. I wasn't as strong-willed and assertive
(family translation: pigheaded) as Katie, who'd inherited the bossiness of that legendary Aunt Kate
for whom she'd been named. I was "that nice little
Albright girl," which explained why at ten minutes
after three I was standing with forced politeness

while Mr. Dirksen told me in precise detail what he thought of my shortcomings on my last Latin test.

"I'm sure your aunt, Miss Albright, would be glad to help you if you asked her," he finished acidly.

I did not need this, on top of having discovered in English class that Miss Olsen was spending this marking period on *The Merchant of Venice* and extensive forays into composition. "I know *you'll* do well," she said gaily, handing me a list of the assignments I'd already missed. I bit back the temptation to remind her that Aunt Tish was the writer in the family and not I.

Katie was waiting to walk home with me, and Katie kept waiting could have a caustic tongue. So I hurried down the hall, once Mr. Dirksen finished his lecture. Katie is not only my dearest friend, she is also, incongruously, my aunt, and being ten months my senior is very much in the habit of acting like Big Sister. I can understand why. Katie suffers from being kid sister to six siblings who range from my mother through Uncle Ben the lawyer, Aunt Tish the writer, and Aunt Marnie the ex-tomboy, now the mother of four boys. Not to mention Peter the zoologist and Melissa, who, as Gram says, "majored in boys and foolishness" in school. All exuberant and opinionated; all (except Tish who lives in England) living within a few blocks of each other. They helped Gram and Gramp bring Katie up—and Katie, having nobody younger in her own house to boss, instinctively does to me as she's been done to. I can understand it, but that doesn't always make it easier to put up with.

The girls' cloakroom was empty, which meant Katie must be already at the door. Nonetheless, I stole a moment for a swift survey in the mirror. I had hoped my week's incarceration might have left me looking interestingly pale and fragile, but the mirror told me clearly that I was still plain Saranne Albright, with the dark hair that refused to wave, and the sprinkling of freckles on the sallow skin. When reporters describe Aunt Tish, who inherited this same complexion, they refer to it as olive-gold and make it sound romantic. It's wonderful how fame can turn a liability into an asset.

"Kid, aren't you ever coming?" Katie's face loomed behind mine in the mirror. "Come on, the meeting must have already started!"

"What meeting?"

"Browning Society. Weren't you listening at the lunch table?"

"I thought all we talked about at lunch was your birthday party. And I thought I missed a Browning meeting just last week."

"You did. This is special to make plans for Friday night."

I looked at Katie blankly, and she shook her head and thrust a handbill at me. I stared at it, and for a moment the room spun.

!!! BROWNING SOCIETY OPEN MEETING
FRIDAY NIGHT !!!
Public Invited!
Debate—Refreshments—Social Hour!
The Changing Role of Women, in Literature and
Life—Natural or Unnatural?

DEBATE between MARK SCHERMERHORN
SCHUYLER III of Browning Society
and noted alumna
BRONWYN STERLING ALBRIGHT!!!

MSS III, Congressman Schuyler's son, new to our school this fall and promptly elected president of Browning Society in this, his senior year, happens to have an old-fashioned sense of masculine superiority . . . and to be the only reason I wanted to be in Browning Society at all. And Bronwyn Albright, past Browning President, noted suffragette and public speaker, wife of the prominent attorney, happens to be my mother.

"I gather you didn't know," Katie said drily, and then, with concern, "Saranne, are you all right?"

"I'm fine," I said, with as much dignity as I could manage.

"I'm surprised Bron didn't tell you."

"She probably forgot. I was sick all last week, remember? And on Sunday, when we ate at your house, all anybody talked about was your party, and Melissa's flirting, and the War, and how we haven't heard from Aunt Tish for months. Besides, Mother doesn't realize it embarrasses me sometimes to have her so—notorious. And don't you dare go telling her, Katie Sterling!"

* * *

I was very conscious of the ticking of clocks all that day. They brought lunchtime, where everyone talked about the debate. Three o'clock; home from school with a Katie, who seemed not herself, alternately a chatterbox and silent. Four o'clock, tea at the kitchen table and having to be polite when Aunt Sadie plunked herself down to brief Mother on arguments for the debate. Hating myself for being resentful of Aunt Sadie's disparaging contempt toward the "young whippersnapper"; for wishing Aunt Sadie wasn't going with us tonight; for not wanting to be identified before . . . people

. . . as Sourpuss Sadie's niece, Bronwyn Albright's daughter.

Five o'clock, cooking dinner so Mother could work her nervous energies off in private. Five-thirty, dishing up, seeing Mother emerge from her bedroom radiant in coral silk. Seeing Dad gaze at her with pride. Wondering if . . . somebody . . . would ever, *could* ever look at me like that.

Seven o'clock, walking to the high school, being introduced to Mark's parents by my father, who knows everyone. Mark's father, like a matinee idol, all tanned skin and gleaming teeth. Mark in a suit I hadn't seen before, which made him look like a college junior. Katie, with her hair pinned up by one of Melissa's Spanish combs, whispering, "I got out of the house before Mama saw me. She won't make a scene in public, so she's livid, but at least I'm safe!"

Gram like a brisk bird, eyes bright, torn between indignation at Katie and pride in my mother. Gramps and Dad, who were best friends long before being in-laws, beaming with pride. Family all over the place—the Sterlings and the Albrights were out in force, all except Aunt Tish, who was across a war-tossed sea.

I wondered why I was suddenly thinking in phrases that could have come from one of Aunt Tish's novels. But I didn't have to wonder about my turbulence of feelings. I didn't want Mother to fail in her debate. But I didn't want Mark Schuyler to fail either!